7/31/19
15.95

HATEFUL THINGS

TERRY GOODKIND is a number one *New York Times* bestselling author. His Sword of Truth series has sold over 20 million copies. Before writing full-time, Terry worked as a wildlife artist, a cabinetmaker and a violin maker. He writes thrillers as well as epic fantasy and lives in the desert in Nevada.

BY TERRY GOODKIND

THE SWORD OF TRUTH SERIES

Wizard's First Rule
Stone of Tears
Blood of the Fold
Temple of the Winds
Soul of the Fire
Faith of the Fallen
The Pillars of Creation
Naked Empire
Debt of Bones
Chainfire
Phantom
Confessor
The Omen Machine
The First Confessor
The Third Kingdom
Severed Souls
Warheart

THE CHILDREN OF D'HARA

The Scribbly Man
Hateful Things

THE NICCI CHRONICLES

Death's Mistress
Shroud of Eternity
Siege of Stone

THE ANGELA CONSTANTINE SERIES

Trouble's Child
The Girl in the Moon
Crazy Wanda

The Law of Nines

TERRY GOODKIND

HATEFUL THINGS

A Children of D'Hara Novella

Episode 2

HEAD
of
ZEUS

First published by Head of Zeus in 2019

975312468

A catalogue record for this book is available from the
British Library.

ISBN (HB): 9781789541205
ISBN (E): 9781789541199

Printed and bound by CPI Group (UK) Ltd,
Croydon, CR0 4YY

Head of Zeus Ltd
First Floor East
5–8 Hardwick Street
London EC1R 4RG
WWW.HEADOFZEUS.COM

HATEFUL THINGS

1

"A boy and a girl?" Kahlan asked in astonishment.

"Yes, that's right," Shale said with a single nod and a warm smile. "You are pregnant with twins."

Kahlan stared up with both excitement and a deep sense of dread. Having twins—a boy and a girl—would be like a gift from the good spirits. It was a way for Richard's gift and her Confessor power to live on into future generations. The House of Rahl would not die out. The lineage of Confessors would not end. It couldn't be more perfect.

Kahlan winced as she tried to sit up. She put an arm across her abdomen to comfort the unexpected pain of the attempt.

"Easy," Shale said, pressing a hand against Kahlan's shoulder to ease her back down. "Your injuries were life-threatening, and you've only just been healed, at least for the most part. Your body is still in the process of completing the final repair of those injuries. Your muscles have been tested to exhaustion. You need to rest to complete your recovery."

Kahlan put her hand over Shale's in gratitude for saving her life after she had been attacked. She had worked tirelessly to keep Kahlan from dying or losing the use of her arm.

Even though she was a sorceress, the woman looked entirely too young and beautiful to be so accomplished a healer. Her youthful beauty laid over a shadow of wisdom and authority—that odd combination of freshly bloomed femininity and seasoned shrewdness—gave Kahlan pause in the back of her mind that Shale was more than what was on the surface.

At the moment, though, Kahlan was tormented by bigger issues than the hints of things beyond the woman's beauty or her own mortality. She gently pushed Shale's arm aside as she sat up and swung her feet down off the bed. She finally stood. Shale, sitting on the edge of the bed, rose up beside her, ready to steady her or catch her if her legs gave out. Kahlan willed herself to straighten up. She found that she felt better being on her feet.

The lavish bedroom was still and quiet, lit only by the soft glow of lamps and a low fire in the massive fireplace. Kahlan knew that most of the Mord-Sith would be out in the entryway guarding the bedroom. She knew that Vika, though, would be guarding Richard.

With the Mord-Sith standing guard outside and Shale in the room with her, the private sanctuary seemed safe enough. But the thing that had attacked and nearly killed Kahlan hadn't needed to come through the doors. After all, it had attacked her when she had been in a locked room. From that, it seemed that those mysterious predators could appear anywhere.

Weighed down by the worry of the new threat to their lives and their world, Kahlan slipped on a robe and then opened the double glass doors to the balcony. The Lord Rahl's quarters for countless generations—now her and Richard's bedroom—were high up in the People's Palace and heavily protected by the men of the First File, the Lord Rahl's personal guard. At the far edge of the balcony, the fluted white marble balusters and railings had wild black veins among gold flecks. The grand balcony jutted out far enough over the edge of the plateau for her to be able to stand at that railing and look down past the palace to the Azrith Plain far below.

Kahlan tightened her robe against the chill. Summer was drawing to a close. The cold was a harbinger of the harsh times ahead.

In the predawn darkness there was no view of the Azrith Plain. Many times, beneath the vast sky it was a beautiful sight, in a stark, barren sort of way. It was a view of the world without the robes of green hills, carpets of forests, or jeweled streams of sparkling water. Instead, it was rather pure in the honesty of its unadorned form.

In a way, it was a visual reminder of how cruel and unforgiving the world of life could be beneath the façade of beauty.

Now, though, there was nothing to see except when lightning flickered. The lamplight coming from the bedroom behind her illuminated falling sheets of rain.

It was a gloomy, foreboding view that matched her mood.

Kahlan wanted these two children—Richard's children—more than anything. She had known she was pregnant, but to learn that she was pregnant with twins nearly took her breath with the unexpected excitement of it. As much as she wanted these children, though, she didn't know if she could dare to hope that she would ever have them.

The sorceress came up from behind. "Winter has already come to the Northern Waste. It will be down here soon enough."

"Is that where you are from?" Kahlan asked, her mind sinking into cold, dark thoughts.

Shale nodded as she gently placed a hand on Kahlan's shoulder. "I know your concerns and fears," she said as if reading Kahlan's mind, "but these children, the continuation of Lord Rahl's gift and your power, are what will help keep our world safe into the future. This could not come at a better time."

Kahlan folded her arms. "It could not come at a worse time. Giving birth to them will only mean that they would be hunted and slaughtered by the Golden Goddess and her kind. Our world needs them, needs our lines of magic to continue in order to protect our people into the future, but for that reason the Golden Goddess cannot allow them to live." Kahlan stared out into the darkness. "She will come for them."

"Are you saying that you would seek out an herb woman who would murder those unborn children in your womb before the Golden Goddess can?"

Kahlan recoiled at the very notion of ending the lives of her two unborn children before they could be born. But that dark thought, not fully formed, had been lurking in the corner of her mind. The way Shale had framed it was starkly cruel, and it was, but still, Kahlan couldn't help wondering about the mercy of such an act.

A cold tear ran down her cheek. "I didn't say that."

"Mother Confessor, your pregnancy is a joyous thing. Having these two children will preserve Lord Rahl's gift into the future. It would mean that you don't have to be the last Confessor."

"There is no way to know if either of these two children would carry our gift. They could be skips. Magic does not always pass on to the children of the gifted. It frequently skips one generation, or even many generations."

Even as she said it, she knew that daughters of Confessors were always born Confessors. But not all the sons of the Lord Rahl were born wizards.

"And if they are gifted? If it is what is needed for magic to continue to be the link that protects our world?"

Kahlan wiped the tear from her cheek as she looked back over her shoulder. "What if they are not gifted? Then having these children would not preserve magic in our world. Though it would be my greatest joy to bear Richard's children and they would be loved no less, they may not be gifted. If they aren't, and especially if they are, they could only look forward to being born into a dying world preyed upon by the Golden Goddess and her kind with no hope for the future."

Shale showed a curious smile. "I don't believe the good spirits would play such a cruel trick at such a time of need."

"How can you be so confident?"

Shale's smile widened as she placed her hand against Kahlan's belly. "Because I can feel it in them."

Kahlan's eyes widened. "You can say for sure that they are gifted? Both of them?"

Shale nodded with conviction. "I can."

Kahlan looked away again, out into the darkness. While that was what their world needed in the long term, it only made the immediate situation far worse.

The Golden Goddess would be able to see their magic. She called Richard the shiny man because she could see his magic shining in him. These two unborn children of D'Hara would draw that evil to them.

For all she knew, the goddess could sense that magic growing in Kahlan's womb at that very moment and could very well already be coming to kill her. It occurred to her that the goddess had already sent her kind to kill Kahlan and these unborn children. Kahlan had barely escaped alive. The goddess would send others to finish the job.

They would not be so timid the next time.

"This is not the way I wanted it to be," Kahlan said in a whisper. "Any time but now. Even if by a miracle these children are born, their birth will be their death sentence."

2

"Mother Confessor, don't you say 'Rise, my child' to any who fall to the ground at your feet?"

Kahlan stared out at the sheets of rain gently billowing in the breeze. "I do."

"So, all people are in a way the children of the Mother Confessor, are they not?"

Kahlan absently nodded in answer.

"Your instinct, as the Mother Confessor, is to protect your people—your children, is it not? Isn't that in a way the whole point of that singular title?"

"It is," Kahlan said.

"And you just fought a long and terrible war to protect them all, did you not?"

Kahlan nodded again, not knowing what the

sorceress was getting at. "It was a terrible war. A long and terrible war. But for life to prevail, I had no choice but to fight. My whole life I have been in one endless fight to protect people from evil."

"And now you must continue to fight to protect all your children, especially the ones growing in you, even though they are yet unborn."

Kahlan took a deep breath and let it out slowly as she turned back to face the sorceress.

"This is different. These children would never have a chance at life. They will be killed for who and what they are. The Golden Goddess has everything on her side. She will not give up. She has vowed that magic will end in this world, one way or another, and when it does, her hordes will hunt us to extinction."

Kahlan couldn't stand the thought of bringing these two new lives into the world only to subject them to the terror of being slaughtered by such relentless evil. She ached with fear and dread for them.

"They hardly have everything on their side," Shale scoffed.

Kahlan frowned. "What are you talking about? You heard what Nolo said."

"Richard is a war wizard. He will fight to stop the Golden Goddess and her race of predators. War wizards are born with that power, that gift, expressly to face threats, both those known and those unknown. His children carry that gift. The world needs them."

Kahlan slowly shook her head. "You don't understand. There is more to it. The Golden Goddess is not the only threat. There is another that in some ways is just as formidable."

Shale leaned in to rest her fingers on the baluster while searching Kahlan's eyes. "What are you talking about?"

Kahlan drew a hand back across her face, wiping away the tears. "I'm talking about Shota."

"Shota?" Shale's nose wrinkled. "Who is Shota?"

Kahlan pressed her lips tight for a moment before answering.

"Shota is a witch woman."

One of Shale's eyebrows lifted. "A witch woman?"

Kahlan nodded. "When Richard and I first met her, she put snakes all over me."

Shale looked puzzled. "Snakes? Why?"

"To keep me from moving and getting close

enough to use my power on her. Back then I needed to physically touch a person to take them with my power. I no longer have to be close. My power can now span such a distance, but back then it couldn't, so Shota wanted to keep me at a safe distance from her, and she knew how afraid I am of snakes. She said that if I moved, those vipers would bite me. She intended in the end for those venomous snakes to kill me."

"Had you threatened her?"

"No."

Shale looked even more perplexed. "Then why in the world would a witch woman want to kill you?"

Kahlan gestured, as if weakly trying to banish the awful memory.

"She said that if she were to let me live and Richard and I ever had a child, it would be a monster."

Shale looked even more puzzled. "What would give her that idea?"

Kahlan let out a deep sigh. "In the distant past there were dark times caused by male Confessors. The gift passed on from a Confessor mother would give these male Confessors extraordinary abilities and power. That Confessor power alone corrupted them, and they used it to gain power. They were brutes who cast the world into tyranny and terror.

"Because of that history, at birth any male born to a Confessor is killed. That awful duty fell to the father. It had always been that a Confessor took her mate with her power so that he would not hesitate to carry out those instructions. Fortunately, males born to Confessors became rarer over time, so such infanticide became rare. Richard is the first one to love a Confessor and not be taken by her power.

"Because he is not bonded to me in that way, but by love, Shota knew that Richard would never kill any child of mine. He admitted to her that he could never do such a thing."

"Does the power of a Confessor pass on to all female children?"

"Yes. Every daughter born of a Confessor is herself a Confessor. It's the way the power was infused into us when originally created by a wizard named Merritt. The first Confessor, the one he created, was Magda Searus."

"Are the male children also always born with the Confessor power?"

Kahlan bit her lower lip as she squinted into her memory. "I guess I can't say for sure. It was a long time ago. It could be that only some were born with the Confessor ability, but the ones who had it certainly caused enough suffering, so the male children of Confessors are never allowed to live."

"Then Shota's worry may be for nothing. Your son may not have that ability. He may have only Richard's gift. Since Confessors rarely have male children, it is likely the girl has your power, and the boy Richard's. Besides, even if he has that ability, you both would teach him to be a good person."

"Well, male Confessor or not, Shota said that if Richard and I have a child, it will have both my power and his, and as a result it would be a monster."

"So, she was going to use snakes to kill you? Seems like a lot of effort."

"She did it because snakes terrify me. She couldn't be reasoned with. She is convinced that everyone in the world will be terrorized by any child of ours. She wanted me to feel that kind of terror before I died.

"Richard made her stop. I hate snakes, but

I can't say that I think much of witch women, either, although I have known other witch women who have helped me. One in particular, Red, helped save Richard, but I think that was largely out of concern for her own hide. Witch women are dangerous and nearly impossible to reason with."

Shale grinned as if at a joke only she knew.

"What?" Kahlan asked. "Something funny about that?"

"In a way," she said, cryptically. "Go on."

"Well, anyway, Shota vowed to kill any child of ours. She said the mixing of gifts would create a monster. You have just told me that my twins are gifted—with Richard's gift and with mine. Shota is right about that much of it."

"Witches aren't always right in quite the way you expect."

"Believe me, I know that well enough, but Shota has vowed to kill any children we have. Given the dark history, I guess I can't say that her fears of a male Confessor are unfounded. When I first realized that I was pregnant, there were nights I lay awake, haunted by the fear Shota's words had planted in my mind, that our child would be a monster."

Shale shrugged. "Look at it this way: since you are having twins, a boy and a girl, the boy will likely have Richard's gift, and the girl will be a Confessor. No mixing of gifts. No monster. See? Of all the things you have to fear, that shouldn't be one of them."

"Can you say for sure that the boy won't have both powers? Can you say that the girl won't? Can you promise me that?"

Shale hesitated. "I admit that I am not able to tell that much. I only know that they are both gifted."

"Well," Kahlan said, leaning close, "Shota will not wait to find out. She will simply come to see them dead. She only agreed to Richard's demand that she let me live on the condition that we don't have children. Richard never agreed to her demand.

"Because he never agreed to her demand, she warned him that she would kill me and the child if I ever became pregnant. Even if I do live long enough to give birth to them, she will come after these children and kill them both. She will be relentless.

"Shota is a witch woman. She knows things. She finds out things. I don't know how, but she does. For all I know, maybe she reads things in the stars."

"The stars are now in a different place in the sky," Shale reminded her.

"Yes, well, if I know Shota, she will somehow come to know that I'm pregnant with Richard's children. Shota made it abundantly clear that she believes mixing different gifts creates monsters." Kahlan leaned toward the sorceress to make her point. "You don't know what witch women are like."

Shale cocked her head as she narrowed her eyes. "What do you mean?"

"Well, for one thing, they are profoundly dangerous."

Shale's face didn't reveal what she might be thinking. "Is that so?"

"Yes."

Kahlan felt something brushing against her ankle. She looked down and froze.

There was a large white snake hissing, red tongue flicking the air, curling its fat body around her ankles, locking them together as it flexed and contracted.

Kahlan's gaze shot up to Shale. "You're a witch woman?"

Shale smiled in a way that Kahlan didn't like.
Now she understood that mysterious shadow
of something behind the beauty.

3

"Indeed I am."

Kahlan's eyes widened. "That's not possible. You're a sorceress."

"My father had the gift. He was a wizard. My mother was a witch woman. My father's gift passed down to make me a sorceress, my mother's makes me a witch woman. I am both."

"I've never heard of such a thing," Kahlan said, her eyes still wide.

"Besides the fact that fewer and fewer gifted people were being born, making the gifted rarer all the time, the House of Rahl periodically purged D'Hara of the threat purportedly posed by the gifted still remaining. Richard's father, Darken Rahl, was one of the worst of the lot. He denounced the gifted as criminals and called

19

for them to be eliminated for the good of all."

Kahlan, of course, knew all that. Darken Rahl viewed anyone gifted as a potential threat to his rule. It was, in fact, why she had crossed the boundary into Westland looking for help to stop him. That was how she met Richard.

"Darken Rahl found a way through the boundary and put the Midlands, my people, under the boot of his tyranny," Kahlan said. "He killed any gifted he could find. He hunted down and killed all the Confessors. Only I escaped. That made me the last of the Confessor line."

"That man terrorized the gifted of every kind," Shale said with a sad nod.

"So how did your parents escape his grasp?"

"They fled in fear for their lives and the life of their unborn child." Shale smiled in a sly manner. "The House of Rahl never went looking for such gifted people in the Northern Waste; it was too far away and too sparsely populated for him to bother with. Because Darken Rahl was preoccupied with his war to take over the world, populated areas were where his attention was focused, not such remote and useless places as the Northern Waste. My parents lived there in peaceful isolation, and there they had me.

"In me, their two abilities mixed together to make me both a sorceress and a witch woman. Two gifts mixed together." She leaned a little closer. "A monster, as you described it."

Kahlan forced herself not to look down at the snake compressing her ankles, preventing her from moving. "That's what Shota called such people, not me, and she was only talking about any child that Richard and I would have. She was talking about our gifts being mixed."

Shale's tone took on the quality of an interrogation. "So then, unlike most people, you don't think me a monster because I have two different gifts mixed together?" She arched an eyebrow. "Or think I'm trouble because I am a witch woman?"

"Of course not."

"Are you sure of that?"

"You saved my life," Kahlan said. "You didn't have to get involved. You didn't have to work as hard as you did to save me. You could have let me die and no one would be the wiser. You have proven you are no monster by your actions.

"My children wouldn't be, either, just because a wizard is their father and a Confessor their mother."

"Well, while you are right that witch women are quite dangerous, I am one witch woman who wants you to have those children. Just as my parents fled the tyranny of Richard's ancestors who tried to eliminate the gifted, I, too, want to live in a world where magic exists, a world where we all, despite the unique nature of our individual abilities, can have a future without a fear of being persecuted for who and what we are. A world at peace."

"That's what Richard and I want as well. You lived far removed from the war just ended, but that is what we both have fought so hard for, what we have both been committed to, in fact what the D'Haran Empire is all about."

"That's reassuring to hear." Shale didn't sound completely convinced. "But for that to happen you must have these children. They are the hope for magic to survive in our world, and in turn, for our way of life to survive. You must see to it that they grow and carry your power and Richard's gift into the future."

Kahlan felt relieved by at least that much of it, but the snake around her ankles had her not only unable to move, but afraid to try. She did her best not to think about that fat snake squeezing her ankles, even though she could feel the cold scales sliding across her bare skin.

"You are more than a sorceress and a witch woman. You are Shale. Without you I would have died, and the hope of passing our gifts on to future generations would have died with me. I would like very much for you to see my children not only when they are born, but when they grow into their power."

Shale's intense look finally eased, and she nodded. "Ah. Well then, I guess the snake needs to go."

"I think that would be for the best." Kahlan swallowed. "If I die of fright, I won't be able to have any children."

Shale let out a soft laugh. She gently rolled her hand to the side while bowing her head as if suggesting Kahlan look again. Kahlan glanced down. The fat white snake was gone. She let out a deep sigh of relief.

She didn't know if witch women could make real things appear, or if they only made you believe they were there. She knew that Shota could change her appearance as well as make things appear. There was no way to know what she actually looked like, or if you were looking at the real Shota. For that matter, now she didn't know if she was looking at the real Shale. That might explain the beauty overlaying the ageless wisdom. But Kahlan did know that Shota's snakes, at least, were real enough that their venom would have killed her.

With a finger, Shale lifted Kahlan's chin.

"It wasn't my intent to threaten you or frighten you. I simply wanted you to see that just because that witch woman, Shota, said that mixing magic creates monsters, that is not necessarily true."

"I think that sometimes it results in someone quite remarkable," Kahlan said.

"That is what I hoped you would understand. Your children will also be remarkable. I don't want you to let the fear that Shota planted in your mind become large enough to cause you to act on that fear."

"There is enough evil in the world without Shota inventing more from her twisted imagination." Kahlan fixed the sorceress with a determined look. "If Shota threatens my children, it will be the last thing she ever does."

"Good," Shale said with a satisfied smile.

4

Shale's smile left as a more serious look took its place. "But I didn't know that you had such little faith in Richard."

Kahlan frowned at the woman. "What are you talking about? I have total faith in him."

"Richard is the protector of the D'Haran Empire, is he not? His bond to his people and theirs to him is part of our world's protection. He has proven time and time again that he would fight to the death to protect our people."

"I know that," Kahlan said. "What's your point?"

"Well, what means more to him than anything else?"

Kahlan didn't need to think about it. "I do."

"And don't you think he would fight to protect you and your children? Don't you think he will use his gift and do everything in his power to protect them, even before they are born? Don't you think he would prevent this witch woman, Shota, from ever getting near you?"

"Yes, but—"

"Your children would be of one blood, yours and Lord Rahl's together. You must have faith in him to protect you. This is what he was born for. This is his highest calling. We are all in his hands. The Mord-Sith will always be there to protect you. I will be there if you wish it. You need to have faith in him to protect you so that you can worry about those two children."

Kahlan was baffled at what the woman could be getting at. "I do have faith in him. Complete faith."

Shale leaned in a little. "Then he needs to know that you are going to bear his children. You have been hiding it from him. He needs to be told that you are pregnant so that he can protect you."

Kahlan paced to the stone railing, to the very edge of where the rain was falling only an arm's length away. Lightning danced and darted among the roiling clouds, illuminating them from inside and the barren landscape far below in flickering flashes. Occasional distant, deep rumbles of thunder rolled across the plain.

"I will let you stand with me, help protect me, and if possible be there when I give birth," Kahlan said. "But there is one condition."

"What condition?"

"You must not tell Richard that I'm pregnant."

Shale let out a soft chuckle. "I'm afraid that he is going to find out. It's not the kind of thing you can hide."

Kahlan turned back. "For now I can. It won't begin to show for a while yet."

Shale looked confused. "Why would you want to hide this from him? I haven't known Lord Rahl long, but from what I've heard and seen, he would be overjoyed by this news. He would do whatever was needed to protect you and those unborn children."

"That is precisely why he must not know. At least for now. We can't afford to have Richard distracted from his job of protecting our world. He is a war wizard. He needs to find a way to eliminate this new threat from the Golden Goddess and her kind. All our lives—my children's lives—depend on him and what only he can do."

Shale, looking mystified, spread her hands. "But if he knows you are going to have his children, he will fight all the harder to protect them. That's what you want, isn't it—for your children to be protected?"

"That's the point," Kahlan said.

"What point?"

"You don't know Richard. He already feels guilty for letting me go alone to question Nolo. He thinks that what happened was because he wasn't there to protect me, even though he knows that, as a Confessor, a lone man has never been a threat to me before. He wrongly thinks he made a mistake in not protecting me. With me nearly being killed fresh in his memory, he will not want to again make what he feels was a mistake. If I know Richard, I bet that you had a time of it trying to get him to stay out of here so that you could heal me, am I right?"

Shale made a face as she sighed. "That's the truth." She looked a bit embarrassed. "As a matter of fact, when I first met him in the great hall, I told him that he was an idiot for letting you go alone to question Nolo."

"Well, if he knew that I was pregnant, that would only make him more determined to protect me. He would shift his focus away from where it needs to be right now. Protecting me would become his central focus. Don't you see? We can't afford that right now.

"Of course he can do both—protect us from this new threat and protect me, and he will—but if he knew I was pregnant, it would unavoidably split his attention. I have no idea how he will be able to solve this new threat from the Golden Goddess and her kind. That is for him to figure out. For our part, we dare not burden him with the additional worry of me being pregnant."

"But Mother Confessor, sooner or later it is going to become obvious."

"Yes, later," Kahlan said as she put a hand over those children. "But for now, it's not obvious. For now, we must let him do his job of figuring out how to protect our world. Right now, he needs to worry about everyone before it's too late and our children no longer have a world to grow up in."

"You realize, of course, that when he finds out he is going to be angry with you for keeping it from him."

"Better he is angry then, than we all die in the meantime because he is distracted."

Shale's smile returned. "And you will do *your* job of having these children in order to protect our world in the future."

"Yes, of course."

Shale thought it over for a moment before finally sighing. "All right. You have my word. I will not tell him. It will be up to you when you feel the time is right."

Kahlan held up a cautionary finger. "And you can't tell the Mord-Sith, either. I know how incredibly difficult it is to keep anything from Richard. If one of the Mord-Sith knew, he would soon after find out."

Shale rubbed her forehead with her fingertips as she turned and paced off a few strides before turning back. "All right. No one will know but you and me until you decide otherwise."

"Good. Thank you, Shale."

"But I hope you are prepared for how angry and upset he will be when he learns you have been hiding it from him."

Kahlan flashed a lopsided smile. "I'm not afraid of the big guy. I will smooth his ruffled feathers when the time comes."

5

Holding the scabbard and baldric together in one hand, Richard pulled open the bedroom door. When he did, Vika, who had been sitting on the floor leaning against the door, tumbled back inward. She jumped to her feet, quickly rubbing the sleep from her eyes. Holding her arms out to keep him behind her, her single blond braid whipped one way and then the other as she checked all around for any threat. It was obvious to Richard that she had been sitting on the floor, leaning against the door so that he couldn't sneak off without her.

Some of the other Mord-Sith must have warned her about him occasionally doing just that. There had been times when he had deliberately slipped away from Cara or the others, but not without good reason. Of course, to Mord-Sith, whose sworn duty it was to protect him with their lives, there was no such thing as a good reason to go anywhere without them. They didn't realize, or refused to accept, that when he did that it was most often to protect them from dangers they couldn't fathom or handle. The fact that he did worry about their safety was another reason they were so fiercely loyal to him.

"Any word from Shale or Kahlan?"

Vika shook her head. "No, Lord Rahl."

Shale had been healing Kahlan, and she didn't want Richard looking over her shoulder. At her insistence he had gone off to another bedroom to get some sleep. But with his worry over Kahlan, he had gotten precious little rest.

The soldiers, weapons to hand, were all looking off down the hall to Richard's left, ready to protect him from whatever they were concerned about. The men had been standing guard nearby outside the bedroom he had been using, and apparently something down that hallway had brought them in close to his room. Whatever had them on high alert had drawn their swords.

"What was that sound?" he asked as he slipped the leather baldric over his head to lie on his right shoulder. "I thought I heard something."

The commander of the detachment pointed with his sword down the hallway to the side. "We heard an odd sound as well, Lord Rahl, but I'm not exactly sure what it was. I'm pretty sure it wasn't a natural sound, like the creaking of the palace you sometimes hear."

Richard secured his sword at his left hip. The ornate gold and silver of the scabbard gleamed in the lamplight. He knew from the window back in the bedroom he had been sleeping in that it was not yet dawn.

Before he could ask the commander to describe the sound, Richard heard something new, loud and distinct. Even though it was some distance down the hall, it was clear that this time it was a bloodcurdling cry.

Richard immediately took off down the hall toward the source of the shriek. The entire group of big men of the First File abruptly fell in behind him.

Richard raced down an elegant blue and gold carpet of the broad corridor toward the sounds of yet more screams. Without slowing, he made a turn to the right down a narrower hall, following the frantic cries. It was hard to turn on the slippery stone, so he deliberately hit the paneled wall with his left shoulder and rebounded off of it to help him turn the corner down a narrower hall.

Vika shoved men to one side then the other as she pushed and squeezed her way through the cluster of big, heavily armed soldiers in order to get close to Richard. All of the men knew that Vika was Richard's personal guard, so they didn't try to stop her, even though the First File was also his personal guard. None were willing to challenge a Mord-Sith with an Agiel in her fist, especially not one dressed in her red leather.

The First File was the closest line of defense for the Lord Rahl. These men had worked all their lives to earn a place in the First File. They were all powerful men in chain mail and shaped leather armor. They were all experts in every weapon they carried. Each was deadly. They were all the elite of the elite. Each would lay down his life before he allowed trouble to get a look at Richard.

Yet none wanted to disagree with a Mord-Sith who insisted she be closest to Lord Rahl. Like them, like all the Mord-Sith, Vika wanted nothing more than to protect Richard. For the Mord-Sith, their greatest wish was to die in their duty of protecting the Lord Rahl. It was a twisted wish, but then, the Mord-Sith were rather twisted women.

When Richard had released them all from their long history of enforced bondage to the Lord Rahl, they all chose on their own to stay right where they were. If anything, freeing them and giving them their lives back had only made them more devoted to protecting him, now by choice, not a lifetime of training, punishment, and compulsory duty.

The hall they were all racing down, while elegantly paneled with dyed maple, was dimly lit with reflector lamps spaced a good distance apart, leaving a lot of unsettling shadows. Following the sporadic, weak sound of pain and the occasional, otherworldly, echoing bellow, Richard passed dozens of rooms to each side before having to turn down another hall branching off to the left. The thick, dark mass of soldiers flowed through the halls behind him and Vika. The new hall he entered had only one lamp, back near the intersection, so they were all running into growing darkness.

Even before Richard drew his sword, the weapon's magic was calling to him, eager to join with his suddenly awakened anger at the unknown threat. The magic of the blade was impatient to join with the Seeker's fury and taste the blood of the enemy.

Knowing that he was getting closer to the source of the sounds, Richard at last drew his sword. The unique ring of steel as it was pulled free of the scabbard echoed through the confined space. What little light there was seemed to give the black steel a sinister glow.

Now, with that ancient weapon in his fist, there was nothing holding back the power of the sword's magic from flowing into him. Together, his fury and the sword's joined, ready to confront any threat, eager to meet the enemy.

Behind Richard, the soldiers' weapons clanged and jangled. The dim lamplight sent flashes of reflections off them into the darkness.

As they raced onward, darkness closed in around them. It grew hard to see. Even as they rushed ahead, the weak gasps had died out. The footfalls of all the men sounded like rolling thunder echoing through the narrow hallway.

Suddenly, Richard came upon the crumpled form of one of the men of the First File. A quick look told him that the man had been mauled. Great wounds were cut right through the leather breastplate and the man's rib cage, exposing his insides. His arms were shredded to the bone through the chain mail. He had no weapon in his bloody fists.

Richard looked up just in time to see a dark shape in the distance. He couldn't tell what it was, but it was moving away from them. When it paused to look back, Richard could just detect the lamplight from quite a distance behind him reflecting a dim gold color in the eyes of the predator.

Having already taken in the sight as he had approached the downed soldier, he bounded over the man without losing a stride and was off down the hall after the attacker.

The thing was swift and made no sound. In a fleeting moment, it had melted into the darkness. Richard charged down the dark hallway after it, determined not to let it get away.

Vika grabbed his shirt at his shoulder and pulled him to a stop. Her teeth were gritted in anger.

"What do you think you are doing?" she growled.

"I'm going after it!" Richard jerked his shirt free of her grip.

Before he could be off after the attacker again, she hooked an arm around his to keep him from getting away. "No, you are not going after it! It's all dark down there. We don't even know what that thing is. Did you see what it did to that man back there?"

"Yes, the same thing it had started to do to Kahlan. I have to—"

"No you don't! It wants you to follow. It's black as pitch down there. You wouldn't stand a chance."

Richard, as angry as he was about the man being killed, frowned at her. "What do you mean, it wants me to follow?"

Vika gestured angrily back with an arm. "Don't you see? It mauled that man within earshot of where you were sleeping. It wanted to draw you out and down here, into the dark. It wanted you to come after it."

"It could have just appeared in the bedroom and had me there."

"You heard what Nolo said. They want this

world, but they are wary of your gift. They don't understand it. This one wanted to get you to do something stupid so that you would be vulnerable—just as the Mother Confessor was when one of them attacked her.

"They are using your empathy for your people to try to draw you to them. For all we know there could be an ambush down that hallway, waiting in the dark, with the intention of trying to overcome your magic. There could be dozens of them waiting down there to tear you apart."

The commander of the men standing close behind Richard smoothed down his thick beard as he caught his breath. "I think you should listen to her, Lord Rahl. She has a good point. It could have attacked any number of people asleep in the palace without being heard or discovered. Had it done that, we would only later find the remains. This attack on a lone sentry, near your quarters, only makes sense if you see it as a tactic to draw you out."

Vika bowed her head to the commander as if in respect for the man for agreeing with her.

Richard reluctantly forced himself to think through the fog of rage about their words. He had to ram the Sword of Truth back into its scabbard to quench the anger it was feeding into him. He took a settling breath.

Finally, he gave a nod to Vika. "You're right. Thanks for not letting me do something stupid."

"From what I hear from my sisters of the Agiel, that appears to be my full-time job."

Some of the soldiers chuckled.

"All right," Richard said. "Let's hurry and get back to that man to see if there is anything that can be done for him."

The commander gestured back with his sword. "The only thing you can do for him now, Lord Rahl, is to say some words as he is laid to rest. His pain and terror is at last ended. He is in the hands of the good spirits, now."

Richard felt terrible that the man had died guarding him.

"We need to search this hall and see if that thing is still down there," he told the commander. "If it is, we won't be rushing into an ambush. We will corner it. Have some of your men get torches."

Once close to a dozen men rushed back with torches, Richard moved quickly but cautiously on down the hall, looking for the killer. Men searched every room along the way. At each intersection two men were dispatched to scout side routes. The farther they went down the main corridor, the more the corridors branched off.

After a time-consuming, fruitless search, Richard finally brought them all to a stop. "There is no telling where that thing went. But from what Nolo told us, they can simply melt into thin air and go back to their own world. I suspect it's no longer in the palace."

"I'm afraid I have to agree," Vika said. "I think it's gone."

"But to be sure," Richard said, "I want the men to conduct a thorough search. Make sure they are in pairs at a minimum."

The commander nodded. "I will get more men and we will search this entire part of the palace."

Richard raked his fingers back through his hair. "I need to go check on Kahlan." He was still feeling the remnants of the sword's rage crackling through him. It was hard to douse such powerful anger once it had been ignited. "If the sorceress isn't finished healing the Mother Confessor, I will wring her neck."

"I'm sure she is doing her best, Lord Rahl," Vika offered in a quiet voice.

Richard nodded before addressing all the men watching him. "It looks like these predators are ambush hunters. They pick the moment to strike. That means we will always be at a disadvantage. It doesn't matter how big and strong you men are. If they catch you off guard, or alone, you will be like that unfortunate soldier back there—dead before you know what happened."

"Then it would seem prudent," the commander said, "that all men standing guard, no matter where, do not do so alone. There should be at least two men, maybe three, at each post. That way if the enemy jumps one of them, the others can attack it."

Richard sighed as he nodded. "That's the idea. Please see to it. In the meantime, I need to make sure the Mother Confessor is safe."

The commander clapped a fist to his heart. "This way, Lord Rahl."

"While I'm checking on her," Richard said as he started out, "I want all the officers of the First File gathered." He gestured to the left. "There's a devotion square not far away in that

42

direction. There's too many men of the First File to pull them from their duties all over the palace and address them all at once, but by meeting with the officers they can pass my words on to their men. Have them gather there so that I can talk to them."

6

Kahlan, in the white dress of the Mother Confessor, was just emerging from their bedroom as Richard hurried into the entryway from the broad corridor. He could see that her arms were moving without pain. She was walking straight and tall, which told him that the healing had been successful.

When her green-eyed gaze locked on him, her expression brightened.

The Mord-Sith were all gathered in that round entry where they had been guarding the bedroom all night while Shale had finished the healing. Only Vika had gone with Richard to another room where he could get some rest.

A weary-looking Shale followed Kahlan out. Richard knew that such a healing would have been quite an ordeal for her as well as Kahlan. He could read in the sorceress's face and in her aura the toll it had taken on her.

Kahlan rushed into his arms and for a long moment he lost himself in that embrace, relieved beyond words to see her looking like herself again. As he was hugging her, he reached out with one hand to touch Shale's arm in appreciation for what she had done. She returned a proud smile.

"Did you sleep well?" Kahlan asked, holding his upper arms as she pushed back from the hug.

"Without you? Hardly at all."

Kahlan flashed him her special smile. "Now that Shale has finished healing me, tonight you will be back with me, and I will see to it that you do."

"There was an attack," he said, hating to break the spell of her smile.

Just that quick, the smile was gone. "What?"

"I'm pretty sure that it was the same kind of thing that attacked you—one of the predators sent by the Golden Goddess. The thing you called the scribbly man."

Kahlan's face lost some of its color. "Where? When?"

Richard pointed a thumb back over his shoulder. "A short time ago. It was one of the soldiers standing guard by himself down the hall not far from the room where I was sleeping."

"Was he severely hurt, Lord Rahl?" Shale asked from behind Kahlan. "Can I help?"

Richard shook his head. "I'm afraid it's too late to help him."

"Dear spirits, that's terrible." Kahlan frowned. "Why attack a lone man standing guard? That seems odd."

"I think because I was sleeping nearby."

Just then, a soldier of the First File rushed into the entryway breathing heavily. "Lord Rahl, Mother Confessor, are you both all right?"

"Yes," Richard said. "What is it?"

"One of the sentries standing guard down a hallway branching off from this corridor coming in here was just found dead."

"Did it look like he had been mauled by a bear?" Richard asked, his heart sinking.

"That's right," the man said, looking a little surprised. "There is no sign of whatever it was that attacked him."

"So, you didn't catch sight of it?"

"No, Lord Rahl."

"I heard a scream a couple of hours ago," Cassia said.

Richard turned to stare at the Mord-Sith. "And you didn't go to help the man?"

She frowned. "Of course not, Lord Rahl."

"Why not?"

"Because our duty is to protect the Mother Confessor. It could be that it was a diversion to draw us away from protecting her. We are not going to abandon our duty to keep her safe. The risk of doing so would be too great. It is the job of the First File to respond to such things."

Richard looked at the grim faces of Rikka, Nyda, Vale, and Berdine. None looked to think any differently.

"Lord Rahl," Berdine finally said, "we are here, in your place, to protect your wife. She is just as important to preserving the magic protecting this world as you are. I know you would not want us to be tricked into leaving her without our protection. We would not trust her to anyone else's care. We are the last line of defense. We would all die before harm could get a look at her, just as we would all die before harm could get a look at you."

"That's right," Cassia added. "I am sorry one of the men of the First File was killed, but that's all the more reason we should not leave our post guarding the Mother Confessor."

Vika looked to her sister Mord-Sith. "Lord Rahl sometimes gets crazy ideas to expose himself to danger. Fortunately, I was there to stop him from doing something foolish and dangerous only a little while ago, in a similar situation."

The rest of them nodded solemnly.

"Protecting him is often a burden," Berdine confirmed.

Richard was used to the Mord-Sith talking about him in such a way, right in front of him, as if he were a doddering old fool who could barely feed himself.

He turned back to Kahlan, spellbound by her green eyes, but needing to return to business.

"I asked the officers to meet us in a devotion area not far from here," he finally said. "With two men killed already this morning, I'm sure rumors will be circulating among the First File. We need to let them at least know the nature of the threat. We need to come up with a plan to fight it."

"They can appear out of thin air," Kahlan said, sounding skeptical that any planning could be possible.

"I know. That makes it difficult, but we've learned one thing. They are attacking targets around both of us to try to draw us out and into a surprise ambush."

Kahlan looked more than a little concerned. "It seems they can appear anywhere, so why wouldn't they simply attack us right there in our rooms, much like the way they did when I was alone with Nolo? Why not surprise us that way?"

Richard stared off for a moment, trying to reason it out in his own mind. He finally looked back at Kahlan.

"They are afraid of our magic. They tried a direct surprise attack on you when you touched Nolo with your power. They struck when you were at your weakest. Even though that thing ripped into you, I suspect that it vanished before finishing the job because at the same time your power was already returning. Nolo says they are fearful of our magic.

"Before, when Shale was beginning to heal you, I was going down a hallway that was dark because the lamps had gone out. One of them appeared suddenly. I don't know where it came from, or if it came out of nowhere. It was simply suddenly there."

"What did it look like?" Kahlan asked.

"It was too dark to get a good look at it. This dark shape suddenly came rushing at me out of nowhere. I had my sword out before it was on me and I was able to take a swing right through the middle of it."

Kahlan leaned in. "And then what? What happened? Did you kill it?"

Richard shook his head in regret. "Then it just wasn't there, as if it never had been. For just an instant I thought I had only imagined the whole thing, imagined I had seen something in the dark—a shadow or a twist of the light. I wondered if I'd been scared by my own shadow. But I wasn't. Something was there. My magic— the sword's magic—must have scared it off. I suspect they are attacking people around both of us to test the limits of our powers."

"Or to try to test themselves against it," Shale said.

"That could be, too," Richard said in a worried tone as he paced off a few feet, thinking.

"We need to warn people of this new danger," Kahlan said.

"Can people defend themselves against these things," Vika asked, "these scribbly men, as you called them?"

Kahlan shook her head. "No, they can't. No one can, except maybe Richard and maybe me."

"Then what can be accomplished by telling everyone that our world is under attack from an unknown threat that will come out of nowhere to rip them apart and there's nothing they can do to save themselves? That would terrify people, which is exactly what Nolo said these predators seek: terror."

Richard rubbed his chin in thought. "I'm afraid Vika is right."

"Along with the First File, we are the steel against steel," Vika said. "You are the magic against magic, Lord Rahl. This what you were born to do."

"These predators don't have magic," Richard reminded her.

"Well, they have something that enables them to get from their world to ours in order to hunt and kill us. You are the only one who can figure out how to fight beings that can do that."

"Right now, you can't worry about the people living in the palace," Berdine added. "You need to focus on stopping this threat, not managing panicked people."

"They have a point," Kahlan said.

"I'm afraid I have to agree." Richard let out a deep sigh. "The Golden Goddess and her kind are using our empathy for others against us to goad us into traps."

Kahlan shook her head in despair. "What can we do about that?"

Richard's gaze swept over the six women in red leather all standing at ease, watching him. "We have a secret weapon."

Kahlan frowned. "What secret weapon?"

"The Mord-Sith," Richard said with a wry smile. "They have no empathy."

The Mord-Sith all flashed self-satisfied grins.

7

Richard watched a school of gold-colored fish in a loose group gliding gracefully through the reflecting pool in the center of the devotion square, their long, flowing tails swaying rhythmically side to side as they slowly circled the large, black, pitted boulder sitting in the center of the pond. Vines, with delicate little blue flowers and roots fanning out in the water, grew up along the sides of that boulder, clinging to it, reaching for the light above. It was the way of life, it seemed, to always reach for the light.

The predators that hunted them, though, sought the darkness from where they struck.

Overhead, the roof above the pool was open to a gloomy, gray sky. The heavy rain of the night before had stopped, but by the way the sky looked it could easily start again at any time.

Richard stepped up on the short blue tiled wall that surrounded the square pool, and turned to the dozens of silent officers standing at attention in neat rows before him. Kahlan stood on the floor in front of him to the right. Three of the Mord-Sith stood at ease to her right, three more to Richard's left.

Shale stood off a little farther to the left, hands clasped before her, watching. Her hair, parted in the middle, wasn't nearly as long as Kahlan's, and it was dark, but like Kahlan's it gleamed in the flat light from above. Most of the men hadn't been able to avoid staring at her when they had come into the square. Shale had an arresting presence. She looked both alluring and intimidating at the same time, as if daring men to look at her and threatening them if they did.

Richard knew that was the witch woman in her. Witch women were dangerous. Shale radiated that danger even without intending to do so. For some witch women, like Shota, they intended every bit of that threat and more.

Most of the soldiers standing before them

wore chain mail under shaped leather armor along with broad weapons belts holding at least a sword, a double-bladed axe, or a mace. Many had two weapons, some all three. A few of the men, specialists in close-quarters combat, additionally had metal bands with razor-sharp projections around their arms just above their elbows. Those projections could tear an opponent apart in seconds.

Richard clasped his hands behind his back as he began. "While we are all grateful that the long and terrible war has finally ended, we unfortunately find ourselves facing a new threat unlike anything we have faced before." His expression was grim as terrible memories flashed through his mind. "And we have faced many terrible things before."

He could see the uncertainty on many of the faces. He knew that most of these men would have heard rumors. He wanted to end the rumors with what he knew.

"As I'm sure all of you have noticed, since the end of the war the stars in the night sky look completely different." Richard smiled a little as he gestured up at the opening through the roof. "At least, when you can see them.

"That is one sign that our world has changed in ways that we don't yet understand and can't predict, but what I do know is that somehow we have come within the reach of a new threat from a race of predators from another world. Their leader is called the Golden Goddess. They are not human. Their only motivation is to hunt, kill, and eat. To them, we are merely prey. Rabbits before wolves.

"There can be no reasoning with these predators, no treaty, no peace agreement, any more than the rabbits could insist on peace when the wolves are of a different mind. Although I can't yet explain it, they somehow come into our world and when they do, they come for only one reason. They come to kill. So far they quickly vanish back to their own world before we can kill or capture any of them."

"They have magic, then?" Commander Sedlak asked.

"No. In fact, they fear magic, or at least they're wary of it. That's why I want the tradition of devotions to continue. For now, that link to my magic is the only thing keeping them cautious. If they can kill the Mother Confessor and me, then they will no longer have reason to be cautious. They will flood into our world, where they will hunt humans to extinction."

"What do they look like?" another man asked. "Are they like wolves, or gar, or something like dragons?"

Richard shook his head in regret. "No one has seen what they look like. At least, no one who has lived to tell about it. I think they walk on two feet, although I can't yet say for sure. We know they have claws or talons that can rip a man to shreds. I'm sure you have heard about the men who have been killed. That is how they died."

Lieutenant Dolan lifted a hand, and when Richard nodded asked, "How do we fight them? Can they be harmed by our weapons?"

"Since they don't have magic, I would assume so," Richard said. "The problem is seeing them in time, and then reacting before they can strike or vanish back into their world. But they often eat what they kill. That means they are living creatures. If they are living, then they can die. Our job is to kill them—you men with steel, me, with magic. I intend to find a way that I can do just that. In the meantime, the First File is our first line of defense, here, at the palace.

"So far, because they are being cautious, they seem to favor using the cover of darkness and ambush. That means they are thinking creatures. We need to outthink them. I want all of you officers to convey what I am telling you to all of your men. We need all of the First File to understand what we know so far about the nature of what we face. Once I find out more, I will let you know.

"Because they strike so fast, I want no man patrolling or standing watch alone. There should always be at least two men on watches and when patrolling. Groups, when possible, would be even better.

"While I want you to spread the word among your men, I don't want any of you or your men to tell anyone else about this. That means those living in the palace and those visiting delegations who are in the process of departing. For now, this is privileged information for men of the First File alone."

Lieutenant Dolan frowned with concern. "You don't want us to warn people about a threat that could come out of nowhere to attack them?"

"And what good would that do?" Richard asked. "Right now, there is nothing people can do to keep themselves safe. That's our responsibility. Even locking themselves in their rooms won't help, because these predators can appear out of thin air right in those rooms. Telling people would only spread panic throughout the palace, and that would cause people to flee. These creatures are predators. Predators are driven to chase running prey. From what I know, there is nowhere safe, nowhere to run, nowhere to hide. Whether here at the palace, or in a far distant land, everyone is prey for this race of predators.

"As more attacks happen, there will soon enough be panic. But for now, our duty is to try to find a way to stop this menace, not scare the wits out of everyone without being able to offer a solution.

"For now, I believe the primary goal of these creatures is to kill the Mother Confessor and me so that our magic won't interfere with them marauding unchecked across our world. Not that they won't attack other people—there have been people killed in distant places—but I think those protecting us are likely to be their primary targets."

The bell atop the rock in the center of the pool rang, the first of three, calling everyone to devotion. As that sound reverberated through the palace, Kahlan signaled to Richard that she wanted to say something. He gave her a hand up onto the wall beside him.

All eyes were upon Kahlan, standing tall and proud in the satiny white dress of the Mother Confessor. "I regret more than any of you could ever know, having to call upon you men to fight again. Know that it is not by choice.

"Once again, we must fight for our lives and to protect the lives of our people."

As beautiful as Kahlan was, as intelligent, as kind, as wise, there was no one more ruthless in battle. These men all knew that. Many had fought under her command and followed her into bloody battle after bloody battle. For that reason, more than any other, she held a special place in the hearts of these soldiers. Silence hung over the gloomy devotion square as they waited for her to go on.

"The Golden Goddess, the leader of these predators, spoke to Lord Rahl and me. She is called the collector of worlds. She wants ours.

"To her kind, killing is a sport. They somehow go to other worlds to hunt and kill other species to extinction. That is the purpose that drives them. They get delight in clawing people apart. Our intelligence draws them as an added challenge for their hunts. They seek to inflict pain and terror.

"One of them ripped into me with its claws and nearly killed me. I barely survived. I can't begin to explain to you the pain and terror of being attacked by one of them."

She slowly shook her head as tears welled up in her eyes.

"These beings also lust to slaughter our children."

The room waited in dead silence as a tear ran down her cheek.

"They are hateful things."

Richard knew she didn't like to show weakness by crying in front of people. Now, she seemed to be having trouble controlling her emotions. She wiped the tear from her cheek, trying to compose herself before going on.

"We have no choice but to kill every last one of them, because if we don't, they will not stop until they have hunted us all to extinction.

"In the past have I asked some of you men to bring me the ears of the enemy. This time . . ."

Kahlan gritted her teeth for a moment, the steel coming back to her voice. "This time, I want you to bring me the heads of these hateful things!"

With their fists raised in the air, a deafening war cry rose up from the men, reverberating through the devotion square.

8

Other people from the palace, after the second bell calling them to the devotion, began filtering into the square. At the third bell, along with the Mord-Sith and officers at the front, everyone went to their knees, bowed forward, and placed their foreheads to the ground.

In the hushed silence, as Richard stood watching, everyone in this devotion square and at every other one in the palace began the words they had repeated countless times throughout their lives.

"Master Rahl guide us," everyone said in one, sincere voice. "Master Rahl teach us." Their voices echoed through the stone corridors. "Master Rahl protect us." Those words were like a hot knife through Richard's heart. He didn't know how in the world he was going to protect them. All he knew was that he was the only one who could.

The assembled crowd finished the devotion in that same joined, haunting voice. "In your light we thrive. In your mercy we are sheltered. In your wisdom we are humbled. We live only to serve. Our lives are yours."

This, Richard knew, this bond of his people to him, and him to his people, was what the Golden Goddess feared. It was empathy charged with magic. It bound them together— the people as the steel against steel and the Lord Rahl as the magic against magic. That unity made them stronger. And yet, he didn't know if it was strong enough. What he did know was that this bond was their only hope.

Away from the People's Palace the devotion was spoken once as a reminder, a reinforcement of the bond. But since the palace itself had been constructed in the form of a spell, the power of that spoken devotion was amplified and reinforced. Because of that, at the palace, the seat of power of the Lord Rahl, the devotion was recited three times, three times a day, a reflection of the magical power of nine.

Once the third devotion had ended, Richard signaled Lieutenant Dolan to remain behind as the men went off to inform the rest of the First File of the situation.

"I need to talk to one of the palace officials. Someone who knows about the people living here and about the guests staying here, if possible."

The lieutenant briefly twisted his mouth in thought. He looked from the devotion square off down the adjacent broad corridor.

"This wing of the People's Palace is where the Lord Rahl's quarters are located. It is also the section where the highest officials are located. Those offices are not far from here. I think the man you're looking for is Mr. Burkett. He oversees the administrators of each section of the palace.

"You may remember him from when you met petitioners in the great hall. He was there to help with details." The lieutenant tapped his chin with a finger. "Small chin. All top teeth."

Richard couldn't begin to remember all the people he had met, but he did remember most of the faces of the palace officials. He remembered that face if not the name. He had been an accommodating man, cheerfully helping with all the tedious arrangements and requests of the visiting dignitaries.

While the Lord Rahl issued sweeping orders, it was the palace officials who had to see them carried out. The People's Palace, after all, was more of a busy city atop the plateau than simply a palace. It was home to many thousands, not to mention the thousands more men of the First File.

"I remember him," Richard said with a nod. "Where is his office?"

"Why don't I take you there," Lieutenant Dolan said as he held his hand out in invitation.

Kahlan took Richard's arm as they followed behind the officer. Vika and Shale followed close behind them. The rest of the Mord-Sith, all in their red leather, were swept along in their wake. Richard was sad to see the Mord-Sith no longer in the white leather, as he had asked them to wear in the great hall to signify peacetime. With their red leather on, they now all looked deadly serious, and no longer the least bit peaceful.

The lieutenant led them up a broad staircase made of cream-colored marble. The treads were rounded over on the front edge from all the people who had climbed those stairs through the ages.

On the upper level, they crossed a bridge with short walls capped with speckled granite. Those short walls acted as solid railings to either side. The bridge provided a dizzying view of one of the massive main corridors in the palace. Glassed areas of the roof let the gloomy light filter down to brighten the vast space.

Far below, people going about their business moved along in every direction. Some walked at a leisurely pace, while others hurried. Many of these people lived and worked in the palace. Others had always dreamed of visiting the splendor of the People's Palace. Now that Richard was the Lord Rahl and the world was at peace, they felt it was finally safe to do so.

In places along the sides of the corridor below, there were shops, some with colorful awnings, that sold everything from herbs, to leather goods, to pottery, to trinkets so that visitors could remember their visit to the palace. There were also many different kinds of shops that sold food. There were butchers selling meat, farmers selling vegetables, and people who sold wild things they collected such as herbs and mushrooms. Many of the shops cooked day and night to supply meals. People could get cooked meat on a stick, deep-fried potatoes and fish in paper wrappers, and bowls of stew they ate at small tables right outside the shops. The aromas were intoxicating.

Once they were across the bridge and a short distance down the balcony that overlooked the grand corridor, Lieutenant Dolan finally came to a halt in front of an open doorway. He held his hand out, indicating that this was the place.

Richard rapped with his knuckles on the doorframe as he stepped into the room.

Mr. Burkett was hunched over a sizable desk that looked too small for all the stacks of scrolls, candles, a collection of official seals and sealing wax, and papers of every sort lying every which way. Maps of sections of the palace were pinned to one wall. Another wall held long lists of names.

The man jumped in surprise and then shot to his feet when he saw who it was. His blue-edged robes had three gold bands on the sleeves, marking him as an official of importance. In his haste to stand, he accidentally knocked several scrolls from a pile; they rolled off the side of the desk, then bounced across the floor. One of the open papers fluttered away as if it had flown off in a panic.

"Lord Rahl," the man said, grinning broadly as he tried to catch the paper that had taken flight, "what an honor to have you visit my humble office."

Richard caught the paper as it floated down like a leaf in autumn. He handed it to the man. "Mr. Burkett, I came because I need your help."

Vika squeezed into the room behind Kahlan and Shale. The rest of the Mord-Sith had to wait outside, because there wasn't enough room for them in the small office.

"Anything, Lord Rahl. Anything at all. How can I help?"

"Can you tell me, are there gifted living in the palace?" Richard held a hand out to Kahlan and then to Shale on either side of him. "Present company excluded."

"Yes, of course, Lord Rahl." Mr. Burkett had such a strong overbite that it gave his speech a distinctive, slightly slurred quality. "There are a number of gifted people living in the palace."

Mr. Burkett started rummaging through the

papers on his desk, shoving piles aside as he mumbled to himself. He finally found what he was looking for and yanked it out from under stacks of other papers. He caught a wooden candlestand just before it toppled over. "Yes, here it is. We keep a list. Any gifted visitor is also required to state as much when they arrive so that we can also keep track of them because . . ."

"Because in the past the Lord Rahl was insistent on knowing who around him was gifted," Richard finished for him.

Mr. Burkett cleared his throat. "Yes, well, even though you are the new Lord Rahl and unlike in the past don't harbor animosity toward them, we still keep a list of who they are, as well as where these gifted people live . . ."

"In case their services are needed by the palace?"

The man's face brightened. "Yes, exactly."

Richard frowned. "How many are there?"

Mr. Burkett scratched his scalp as he reviewed the list for a moment. "Actually, Lord Rahl, there are not many. At least not as many as one would expect, considering the size of the palace and the number of people living here."

Richard knew that in the past the People's

Palace could have been a dangerous place for any gifted to live, but its power also drew them.

Mr. Burkett mumbled to himself as he tallied his list. He finally tapped his paper. "There are not quite two dozen gifted living here, Lord Rahl, and one gifted visitor. A gifted woman and her ungifted daughter."

"Good. I need to speak with all of them right away. Could you see to it, please?"

"I have assistants"—the man gestured to the side—"in nearby offices. The palace is quite large, as you know. I can get them right now and we can divide up the task. That way it will help get it done without delay."

"Good. Have them gather at the library here on the top floor." Richard pointed out the doorway, past the Mord-Sith all leaning in watching and listening, to a spot across on the other side of the main corridor. "The one over there, down at the end of that passageway by the white marble column. It's the library with the opaque glass on the doors and windows. There are rather ugly orange-striped chairs just outside, in the sitting area."

Mr. Burkett cocked his head. "You mean the library that is also a containment field?"

Richard was a bit surprised that the man knew what the place was, but then again, he supposed it was his job to know such things.

"Yes, that's the one. Considering the size of the palace I imagine some of the gifted will be quite a distance away, so tell them to meet me there following the afternoon devotion. That should give them time to get there. Tell them I said not to stop for the devotion, but instead get there by the time it's over. It's important that I talk with all of them as soon as possible."

The man bowed, revealing the shiny, bald top of his head with a rather unfortunate liver spot the shape of a daisy.

"Of course, Lord Rahl. It will be done." He hesitated, putting a finger to his lower lip. "Will you be sending soldiers with my men?"

"Soldiers?" Richard was a little puzzled. "No, why?"

"Well, it's just that in the past . . ." the man hesitated for a moment, then cleared his throat, ". . . when the Lord Rahl wanted the gifted rounded up, it often meant bad things, so the soldiers were necessary to make sure they heeded the call."

Richard nodded his understanding. Being

brought to meet Darken Rahl in person was usually cause to be terrified. He knew that from personal experience.

Richard smiled. "Nothing sinister is going to happen to them."

"And if they still don't want to be collected to come meet with you?"

"Tell them that I need their help, that's all."

"And if they still won't come along?"

Richard sighed that the terror Darken Rahl had struck into the gifted still lingered. "Well, I guess if they don't come back here with your assistants, then you will need to have the First File escort them back."

9

As they all emptied out of the cramped office, Mr. Burkett turned toward the offices of his assistants. Richard watched the man hurrying away. He had a hitch to his step that looked like his knees were getting old and ached.

As Richard turned back, he saw a red-faced soldier running along the balcony toward them. He was a big man, with a barrel chest and powerful-looking arms. Richard could see his rank marked on a leather shoulder pad. He came to a stop a little farther away than he had intended when the Mord-Sith closed ranks in front of Richard and Kahlan.

"Lord Rahl, I need to speak with you."

"What's your name, Sergeant?"

He clapped a fist to the leather armor over his heart as he panted, catching his breath. "Sorry. I'm Sergeant Barclay, Lord Rahl. I was in the devotion square when you spoke to the officers. There is trouble and I had wanted to talk to you back there, but then Lieutenant Dolan led you away and you looked like it was important, so I decided to wait until you were finished with Mr. Burkett. I was just checking on my men while you were busy, and then I came back here right away to see if you had finished so I could have a word with you. Lord Rahl, this is important, or I would never think to approach you like this."

"I welcome men of the First File to always feel free come talk to me with important matters, so be at ease, Sergeant. What's the problem?"

He licked his lips nervously. "Well, I'm afraid that we found something. Something you need to see."

Richard frowned. "What did you find?"

"It's down there, Lord Rahl," the sergeant said as he turned and gestured vaguely down over the side of the balcony. He turned back. "I think it would be best if you came to see it for yourself, Lord Rahl."

Richard had important things he needed to do, but this man was clearly quite agitated about something. "All right, but I hope it won't take long."

Sergeant Barclay dipped a quick bow and started leading them all to the grand staircase. Once they were down on the main floor, he took them to a nearby set of plain-looking closed metal double doors. Two soldiers stood to either side, each holding a pike with the butt end planted on the ground. They all wore swords as well. They saluted as one with a fist to their hearts before two of them pulled open the doors for Richard and his group.

Beyond the doors was a service area closed to the general public. Simple hallways led off in each direction, from there to branch off to specific areas. Not far inside the main area was a flight of stairs with a utilitarian iron railing. They all followed as the man hurried down the stairs, two at a time in places. The sound of all their boots in the stairwell reverberated with a hollow echo.

Torches were placed at intervals in iron brackets to the side, creating wavering shadows. At each landing there was a door, presumably to passageways in each of the lower levels. There were two guards posted at each door, at each level, as they descended. The sergeant didn't pause to speak to them as he continued down stairs to ever lower hidden reaches of the palace interior.

Finally, at one of the small landings, the sergeant brought them to a stop. He motioned one of the men standing guard to open the door.

With a concerned look, the sergeant took in the anxious group watching him. "I just wanted you to see this first, so you can get your bearings and know where we are, and what we are near."

Beyond the door they emerged onto a landing in a section of the great inner staircase up to the palace. This inner shaft was how visitors to the palace got up into the palace proper—through the great door at the bottom and then up the interior stairs. The stairs up that interior shaft weren't continuous. The pathway with flights of stairs at intervals meandered along and around the contours and odd shapes of the near vertical walls. There were long flat walkways for stretches in areas. Some of those broad level areas had benches where people could stop and rest.

It was relatively dark in the area where they were standing, but Richard could see silhouettes of people not far off, going up on their way into the palace or going down on their way out. Since the audience in the great hall was over, a great many more people were leaving than arriving.

Much of the interior, being so vast and difficult to light, was dimly lit. There were torches and lamps along the climb to relieve some of the perpetual darkness of the interior underground, but there were also areas, such as the place they stood, where shadowed darkness prevailed. Many people carried simple, inexpensive candle lamps with them that they could buy from vendors along the way. Many did not, and simply skimmed a hand along the metal railing as they made their way across the dark areas.

It was such a long climb up from the Azrith Plain far below that there were shops along the way, carved out of the rock of the plateau in the more expansive level spots. Those shops sold many of the same things as the shops above. Many visitors became discouraged by the arduous climb and would stop at these shops for something to eat, to take a rest, or to buy a souvenir and then go back down.

"How far up is this along the interior passageway?" Richard asked the sergeant.

The sergeant led them back to the service stairwell and motioned the guards to close the door. "Above halfway up. Before, I had a man stationed at each one of these doors on the way down, guarding them so that people couldn't wander in here and have access to the restricted areas of the palace."

"One man at each post?" Richard asked, since there were now two men at each door.

The sergeant wet his lips. "Yes. The doors are always bolted from this side so that people can't wander in here, but we often had men guard the doors when a lot of people were visiting the palace, like now, just so that there wouldn't be funny business. You know how people get curious about locked doors."

Before Richard could question him, the man started out again.

"This way, please, Lord Rahl."

The sergeant continued on down the stairs, hurrying the entire way. After what seemed like an endless series of flights of stairs, they finally approached the bottom. Half a dozen men with torches waited there for them. Even the torches couldn't entirely banish the oppressive darkness. They hissed and sputtered, is if warding off the haunting silence. The smell of burning pitch helped mask the dank, musty odor.

Once Richard and his party had all joined the sergeant at the bottom, the sergeant signaled most of the men with torches to go on ahead. Then he tilted his head, indicating he wanted Richard and the rest of them to keep following as he led them all onward through a wider hall and then a dark passageway that reeked of stagnant water, mold, and dead rats. In places there were puddles of water they had to skirt or step over. Their footsteps echoed in whispers back from the darkness.

When the men with the torches stopped before a broad opening into pitch blackness beyond, Sergeant Barclay halted and turned back to all those following him.

"If it pleases you, Lord Rahl, I think the ladies should remain here while I take you on alone the rest of the way back in there to see it."

"See what?" Shale asked.

"Please, trust me on this." He paused to lick his lips nervously. "If you would, could you just wait here and let Lord Rahl come with me, alone?"

"Where Lord Rahl goes, I go," Vika said with finality.

The other Mord-Sith all looked to be of the same mind.

"You wouldn't have brought us down here if it wasn't something important," Shale said. "I'm going, too."

"Show us what you brought us down here for, would you, please?" Kahlan commanded.

The sergeant was about to object, but at the look of resolve in her eyes, he simply let the breath out and turned to Richard as if to implore him to intervene.

"Just do as she asks, would you, Sergeant?"

The sergeant took one more look around at all the determined faces, then nodded. With a sweep of his arm, he ushered a few of the men with torches ahead into the darkness.

"Watch our backs," he told the ones he left behind. They nodded and took up positions to each side of the entrance.

"What's in here?" Richard asked, wondering what the men needed to watch their backs from. In some of the broader areas Richard saw the shapes of stone blocks stacked in random places. "What is the purpose of this place?"

Sergeant Barclay looked back over one of his broad shoulders as he hurried onward. "It's an area where part of the foundation was constructed. The foundation is massive. I can't say for sure, but I believe this area was used to store construction materials—stone and such—during the construction of the palace. After it was finished the room was left empty, possibly so that the foundation could be inspected from time to time, or possibly it was simply not seen as worth the effort to fill it in."

As they hurried down the roughly hewn passageway, Richard could begin to pick up the unmistakable stench of death. Before long it was bad enough to make his eyes water. Shale and Kahlan tried to cover their mouths, but it wasn't much help.

"Wait," Shale finally said, bringing them all to a halt. "Wait just a moment."

She scooped up a handful of pebbles near the edge of the uneven floor. She spun her other hand around over the top of the hand with the pebbles. Finally, she held out her hand, palm up.

"Here. Each of you take one of these. I infused them with a powerful smell of mint oils. Hold it up to your nose to help keep from gagging." She looked to Kahlan. "In case any of us might have unsettled stomachs to begin with, I don't want any of us vomiting from the smell of death."

The three soldiers, Richard, and Kahlan each gladly took a pebble.

Kahlan held it to her nose and took a deep breath. "I've smelled the stench of death often enough. It's something you never get used to. This helps a little. Thanks."

The sergeant looked grateful for the menthol-scented rock. Richard certainly was. The Mord-Sith seemed indifferent.

Vale took one, smelled it, then handed it back to Shale. "Thanks, but I don't need it."

Shale arched an eyebrow as she glanced at Richard.

Richard didn't feel like taking the time to explain Mord-Sith to Shale. "Let's go," he said to the sergeant.

In a short distance, the smell of death became so overpowering that Richard was glad to have the salvation of the pebble that filled his nostrils with the strong aroma of menthol. It helped mask some of the sickening smell. Without it, it would have been difficult to continue. As it was, it was still hard to take.

The end of the crude passageway opened into a vast chamber. In the dim, flickering torchlight, Richard saw something ahead in the darkness.

"What is that?" He could hear buzzing, but he couldn't see exactly what it was.

Sergeant Barclay held a hand up urging them to wait as he went forward a short distance with a torch to show them what was there. Richard blinked in stunned astonishment when the torchlight lit the scene. Shale leaned forward, her eyes wide.

"Dear spirits help us," Kahlan whispered as her eyes welled up with tears.

10

What Richard was looking at was so incomprehensible that at first, he wasn't sure he could believe that it really was what he thought it was.

There in front of them, up against a dark, towering, rough-hewn stone wall near one of the monolithic footings of the foundation, was a massive pile of remains. It took a moment for it to sink in that the mass of the irregular heap were indeed remains, and that they were all human. Blood and bodily fluids had drained out in great, thick pools across the floor. Clouds of flies buzzed all over the chaotic pile while others drank at the edges of the thick liquid on the floor. In the shadows, what at first looked like the pile moving proved to be rats burrowing through the remains.

The stench was overpowering, even with the menthol stones Shale had made for them. The smell was sickening enough, but the sight of it added another dimension to his revulsion.

White bones or pieces of bones stuck out everywhere from the tangled jumble of spinal columns, smaller bones, clothes, guts, and connective tissue putrefying in the humid darkness. Most of the bones had had small bits of tissue still attached. Bloodstains gave most of the bones a dark patina. Many had been shattered to get at the marrow. Some were gouged with claw marks that Richard recognized from those he had seen on Kahlan's arm.

Here and there Richard spotted chest and shoulder plates from the leather armor of men of the First File. All of them he could see had been ripped apart by claws. That leather armor had afforded no protection from the power of the attackers. Tangled in among the remains were bloody sections of chain mail. Here and there weapons lay among the debris.

There were oozing masses of the dirty ends of viscera that had been tossed on the pile. They almost looked alive as maggots wriggled all through them. Larger bones of legs and arms, and even sections of rib cages, protruded from the continually moving soft mass. Many of the skulls, with rows of white lines gouged down into the bone from teeth that had raked the scalps and faces off of them, had rolled off the pile to litter the floor.

The pile of remains was slightly taller than Richard, and at least a dozen and a half feet across. A quick calculation in his head from the numbers of leg and arm bones, as well as the skulls, told him that these were the remains of possibly several hundred people.

It quickly became clear to Richard what this was.

"They brought their kills down here—or even live captives—to feed off them," he said to the sergeant. "They tossed the bones and things they didn't want to eat on the pile."

Sergeant Barclay nodded. "So it would appear, Lord Rahl."

Kahlan gasped back a sob as she pointed. "Those smaller bones are from children. It's not only adults. There are children among the remains."

A watchful Shale reached a hand out to steady Kahlan.

Richard finally turned his gaze from the horror to look at the sergeant. "How did you find this?"

The man let out a troubled sigh. "A number of my men were approached by people looking for missing loved ones. They helped search and took down the names. I knew something was odd when none of the missing people could be found. Not a one. We often encounter frantic people looking for a lost child or a relative. We almost always find the missing loved ones. But now, we weren't finding any of the missing people, not the missing husbands, not the missing wives, and not the missing children. It was like they all had simply vanished.

"That was strange enough, but then I realized that some of my men were missing as well.

"I started checking and soon discovered who the missing men were."

"Who were they?" Richard asked.

The burly soldier leaned closer. "The thing was, Lord Rahl, the missing men were the ones who were supposed to be guarding the landings on the way down here—the landings with the doors, like the one I showed you. The men had been posted to guard those doors to the inner areas of the plateau where the public comes and goes from the palace. There had only been one man at each post, and now those men were gone.

"So, I took a squad and we went searching. On our way down here, we found bloody handprints here and there, on the corner of hallways, at doorways, even along the walls. It was where the victims were dragged in here, still alive, trying to grab onto a corner or doorway, anything to try to help them get away. None did.

"We kept going, following the bloody smears and the blood that had dripped on the floor." He gestured to the remains. "Eventually we discovered this. I can only imagine how terrified these poor people were as they were dragged in here and eaten alive. Down here, no one would be able to hear their screams.

"I recognized a couple of the pieces of armor. They belonged to my men. Some have a mark that identify their owner. That's how I know who they were and that this was where they had vanished to."

Richard boiled with rage, and at the same time he was heartsick at the discovery. It was especially painful seeing that children were among the remains.

He also felt a rising sense of panic that everyone depended on him to stop this slaughter, and he didn't have the foggiest idea how he was going to do that.

"They were using this place as a base to hunt from." Richard gestured back up the way they had come. "After they killed your men, they used the doors out to the dark landings where people were coming and going from the palace. They were snatching unsuspecting people from the shadows on the landings outside those doorways."

"If ever there was a nightmare come to life, that is it," Kahlan said.

The sergeant nodded. "That was why I wanted to show you the dark landings beyond the doors when we were on our way down here. I wanted you to see where they were likely snatching most of the victims."

Richard took the torch from the sergeant, and alone stepped among the skulls—both of adults and children—scattered on the floor in order to get a closer look at the heap of remains. He had to walk through the sickening pools of blood and fluid. None of the others looked the least bit inclined to want to go with him, except, of course, Vika. She followed closely in his footsteps, her Agiel in her fist, as her analytical gaze swept over the scene.

Richard wanted to get a closer look to burn the full horror of it into his memory so that he would never fail to use every last bit of strength and resolve to stop these hateful things, as Kahlan had called them.

But more importantly, he wanted to see what he could learn about the predators who had done this. He squatted down next to a small skull. It was obviously from a child probably six or seven years old. The scalp and face had been mostly scraped off. Only a little patch of blood-soaked hair remained, above where an ear would have been. With a finger, he turned it around and around to get a better look at it in the torchlight.

The back of the skull was missing. Jagged marks revealed that it had been teeth that had opened the skull, most likely to get at the brains, as the skull was mostly empty.

He bent closer, holding the torch near to see better.

The deep gouges across the top of the skull and down toward the brow were made by a row of many, many sharp, pointed teeth all close together. By the way they were deeper in the center, and lighter and lighter as they moved farther to the side, it told him that the thing had a very large mouth. Only the front teeth had done this damage as they were raked across the bone. He looked around at some of the other skulls littering the floor. They had the same kind of deep gouges raking across the bone, indicating the same thing—a very large mouth with a lot of very sharp, pointed teeth, all close together, tightly lined up across the top and bottom jaws.

Vika shadowed him as he stood and returned to the others, where he handed the torch back to the sergeant.

"What did you learn?" Kahlan asked.

"Without realizing it, they have revealed a little bit about themselves. From the evidence left on the skulls, I can tell that rather than fangs like many predators have that would leave puncture holes, they have a lot of needle-sharp teeth, all about the same length, lined up closely together side by side. Some of the large bones were bitten clean in half, so their jaws are powerful. From the evidence on some of the skulls, it also looks like their mouths are big enough to gnaw on a skull, like we might bite at an apple. From the confusing mass of indistinct footprints, they don't wear boots. From the size of those prints I'd guess they must be half again my size."

"Dear spirits," Kahlan said as she slowly shook her head. "We are in a lot of trouble."

11

They left the site of the slaughter, grateful to be away from the gagging stench of death, and made the long, tiring climb mostly in silence. When they finally reached the uppermost landing of the service stairs, Richard gently grabbed the sergeant's arm and brought him to a halt.

"There is no way we will ever be able to identify all those people. You said you have a list of the names of missing people. I think it's safe to assume that the missing are those we saw down there."

The man nodded. "So, what do you want to do, Lord Rahl?"

Richard felt overwhelmed, frustrated, and angry. "We can't really bring the whole rotting mess back out of there for a proper burial. It would be to no real purpose, since we wouldn't have any way to put the remains of individuals together or identify any of them so that people could grieve and bury their loved one. There is no way we would know who we're burying or if the missing are for sure among them, even though it seems likely that they are. And we certainly can't bring their families down there to the site and tell them that their loved ones are likely among the remains in the pile.

"Seeing those remains would be more horrific to them than the torment of not knowing what happened to their loved ones. There is nothing we could do that would provide closure for people."

"So, what are you thinking?"

Richard wiped a hand across his mouth as he briefly considered. As much as he didn't like the idea of simply leaving the remains down in the lower reaches of the palace, he couldn't see that there was really any choice. There were catacombs under the palace where a great many people were interred. In a way, the victims were already buried underground.

"Their suffering is over. They are with the good spirits, now," Richard finally said to the sergeant. "I'd like you to get a group of men together. Have them collect stone and mortar from down in the lower levels. I saw supplies of that kind down there in some of the nearby rooms off the side passageways. Once you have the supplies you'll need, seal up the entrance to that chamber with the remains.

"Not just a simple wall. Those creatures could probably break through that and go back to using it again. You need to plug up the end of the passageway for a good enough distance that they aren't ever going to be able to break through it to get back in and use it as a nest. That will be the tomb for all those poor victims."

Sergeant Barclay nodded. "Then those creatures will know we are on to them, know we have discovered their lair."

"Good. I want them to know that they aren't as clever as they thought they were. And at least they won't be able to continue to hunt in the same way."

The sergeant tilted his head closer with a serious look. "Lord Rahl, there are many places like that in the lower areas of the palace. They may simply find similar places from which to hunt."

"Of course they will. We will have to be on the lookout for that now that we know what they were doing. We need to quickly deny them places they use wherever we find them. Maybe we can make them feel like the hunted for a change. We might even be able to kill or capture some of them. In the meantime, seal that chamber as a gravesite."

The man clapped his fist to his heart. "I will see to it right away, Lord Rahl."

As the sergeant hurried off through the service area to get a crew to take care of sealing up the tomb, Richard headed in the direction of the double doors that would lead out.

"We need to get up there to meet with the gifted," he told the others. "They likely will be waiting for us by now."

"What are you thinking?" Shale asked, sounding suspicious. "What do you want with the gifted?"

Richard paused before opening the doors out of the service area and turned back to the eight grim female faces watching him. Instead of answering her question, he asked her one. "Do you know how to join gifts from different gifted people to create more power?"

He knew that the Sisters of the Light could do it. He had seen it done.

Shale's smooth brow bunched together a bit. "I've never heard of such a thing. But to be fair, the only gifted people I knew were my parents."

Richard paused in thought for a moment. "That means you may not know how to do what a lot of sorceresses who have been trained are able to do."

Shale's lips pursed with displeasure. "Magic is magic."

"So it is," he said, offering her a small smile.

Kahlan took his arm and pressed her head against his shoulder as he started off toward the grand staircase. He put an arm around her waist and pulled her close as they went up the first flight to the broad landing where the stairs reversed direction to continue on up.

12

Shale hooked a hand around Richard's arm to stop him.

"Lord Rahl . . ." She sounded hesitant. "That sight down there, all those people . . . it was horrifying."

Richard frowned, not knowing if she had a point. "It was."

"Well, the thing is, you hope to be able to stop these predators. In the meantime, our world is steadily heading toward the day when people will be without the protection of your magic and without the Mother Confessor's magic. If anything should happen to either of you, then the future of our world would be doomed as the protective web of your gift holding all magic together disintegrates.

"The Golden Goddess may never send those of her race to have a big battle in which you can hope to defeat her. She may deny you that opportunity of a conventional war and instead continue to attack as she has been, terrorizing us with continual surprise attacks, maybe even wiping out small towns here and there so that everyone will be in the grip of fear. They will continue to feed on our people. As we wait for an attack that may never come, many more people will go missing, just as those people down in the darkness were missing.

"Your magic is the only thing protecting our world by keeping them cautious. The future survival of this world depends on that magic being preserved. Every day that passes increases the danger that you will be killed and our world would then lose that protection.

"As we learned through Nolo, the Golden Goddess can wait us out. If she chooses, she can wait for you to die of old age. You and the Mother Confessor grow older every day, and with your gifts destined to eventually die out, our world gets closer to dying out with you."

Richard was absently wondering what kind of gifted might be living at the palace and what

abilities they might have that would be able
to help them. He was only half listening to
Shale ramble on with the obvious. He realized
that even though she seemed to be talking
a lot without saying much, she was getting at
something.

"What of it? What's your point?" he asked,
impatiently, needing to get to the library where
the gifted would be gathering.

"Well, to keep any of that from happening,
and to have your gifts live on to protect the
future of our world, you and the Mother
Confessor need to have children. It can't wait.
You must have them now."

"Children! Now? Are you out of your mind?"
Richard blew up in anger, flicking a hand
in a gesture toward Kahlan. "I can't think of
anything that could cause us more trouble right
now and threaten to bring the sky down on us
all, than Kahlan getting pregnant."

"But—"

"But nothing! You heard what the goddess
said about the young and how she lusted to
kill them. How can you even suggest that right
now?"

"I can suggest it because every day you both

get older. Just like everyone else, day by day the time when you can have children dwindles away. You must think of the future. You must have children. I think it's time."

"That's absurd. We're hardly old enough to suggest that we are running out of time to have children."

Seeing how angry he was, Shale wisely closed her mouth.

Richard raked his fingers back through his hair, trying to control his temper. "One day? Absolutely. But now? There is nothing that would do more to draw the dedicated ferocity of the Golden Goddess and her kind than us having children." He shook his head at the very idea, almost too angered by to it speak.

Shale's prudence ran out. "But Lord Rahl—"

"Tell her!" he suddenly yelled at Kahlan. "Tell her how that would compromise our situation and in all likelihood ensure the destruction of our world! The entire focus of the Golden Goddess would be to hunt down those children and slaughter them. That would unleash such wrath that it would ensure that Kahlan and I would be killed as well. It would be the end of magic in our world. All because of such a foolish impulse at a time like this. Tell her that we can't put such a notion ahead of us stopping this threat!"

Kahlan had gone pale, making him suddenly wish he hadn't yelled at her. He hadn't really been yelling at her, but rather the recklessness of such a suggestion.

"But Richard—" she said in a small voice, almost a plea.

"Someday, Kahlan," he said, leaning down toward her, softening his voice. "Someday. But right now that is the one thing that could seal our fate and the fate of our world. It would be the single thing that would ensure our total annihilation. Such a thing would cause them to cease being cautious and unleash a full-scale, worldwide invasion. We would be overrun and slaughtered.

"Right now, their attention is on you and me as they probe our powers. Once we can learn more, discover ways to kill them and get control of the situation and hopefully stop them from coming to our world at will, then yes, that's what I want more than anything. But right now we have to use our heads, or we will all lose them like those people down below."

Kahlan nodded as she glanced at Shale. The sorceress had gone silent and red-faced. Richard didn't know what was wrong with the woman to even suggest such a thing right in the middle of such a crisis.

"Kahlan being pregnant would mean that the Golden Goddess could no longer afford to wait us out," he concluded. "Without a way to stop these predators, it would mean the end of us all."

Kahlan turned a look on Shale as she gritted her teeth. "What's the matter with you? Can't you see that Richard is trying his best to figure out how to stop this threat? We don't need to make his job any harder than it already is."

Shale looked a bit sheepish as she abandoned her argument. "I apologize." She gestured vaguely. "I was only trying to broach a subject that one day must be addressed. But I can see that now is not the time." Kahlan closed her eyes a moment as she took a deep breath. "One day it will be. Until then, let's not talk of it again—all right? Richard has a job to do. He doesn't need us to pile more worries on top of those we already have."

Shale's lips pressed tight for a moment.

Finally, she bowed her head. "Of course, you're right, Mother Confessor."

Richard gripped Shale's shoulder and gave it a jostle, along with a smile. "It's a wonderful idea, Shale, just the wrong time, that's all. No hard feelings?"

Shale shook her head, returning a bit of a smile.

Richard held his hand out to Kahlan. "Come on. We need to get up there to see what kind of gifted we have here in the palace. I'm hoping they are strong enough to be able to help us. I'm also hoping that at least one of them knows how to link others with the gift to make it more powerful."

Kahlan took his hand, but stood her ground, making Richard stop and turn to her.

"Richard, I'm feeling a bit sick after what we just saw down below. I think I will go lie down."

Richard was a bit puzzled, even though she did look awfully pale. Kahlan had seen horrific deaths before. It always made her more determined than ever. It was completely unlike her to want to go lie down.

"I don't think that's a good idea right now."

Kahlan frowned. "Why not?"

"Because it's easier for wolves to take down a deer if they can cut one from the herd. Better that we stay together. I don't want you to become one of the missing."

13

Without realizing it, Richard, in his distracted anger, had started taking the stairs two at a time, opening the distance back to most of the others. At a landing where he had to go around a newel post to the next flight of stairs heading up, when the others had lagged a little way behind, only Vika had kept up with him.

With all the shuffling footfalls on the stone steps echoing up and down the stairwell masking her voice, Vika leaned close to whisper to Richard as he slowed to let the others catch up.

"You're right, Lord Rahl, about not needing the additional worry of a pregnant wife and then children in the middle of a fight to try to save all of our lives. I could see that Shale also upset the Mother Confessor. I will tell the sorceress to mind her own business in the future and I will see to it that she does."

Richard, deep in his own thoughts, glanced back at the Mord-Sith. "That isn't necessary."

Vika didn't answer. She simply straightened her back and proceeded up the stairs with him as the others hurried to catch up. Richard knew that it didn't really matter if he told Vika not to say anything to the sorceress. She would do what she thought best to protect him so that he could do what he had to do as First Wizard. Steel against steel so that he could be the magic against magic. That consideration of the larger objective overrode whatever he might say.

Richard was certain that when she caught Shale alone, Vika would deliver a lecture at the end of an Agiel. He didn't want her to do that, but he knew he wasn't going to easily be able to stop that from happening. He also knew that if he tried it would end up causing more drama that he didn't need. He had bigger worries. Besides that, Vika was right. Shale should mind her own business.

He hoped that Shale was wise enough to keep a cool head and not argue with Vika. There were no Mord-Sith in the Northern Waste and Shale had no real idea of how truly dangerous it would be to tangle with one, Vika in particular. While Vika had assigned herself as his personal guard, any of the other Mord-Sith, for that matter, would be just as much trouble to cross. Now that Vika had seen how much Shale had angered him, she had, by extension, also angered Vika.

Such volatile behavior from Vika and her sister Mord-Sith was the price Richard had to pay for having given them their freedom. To the Mord-Sith, such freedom was worthless if they weren't able to exert it as they saw fit. In return for their independence, they protected Richard and Kahlan with their lives. He was beyond grateful for their protection, but at times it tested his patience.

At the head of the stairs, they emerged into a quiet section of the upper level. The top floor of this entire portion of the palace, where the Lord Rahl's quarters were also located, was reserved for the exclusive use of the Lord Rahl and any of his staff he designated as needing access. It was strictly off-limits to the general public. The First File patrolled the area at all times to make certain it was free of any unauthorized visitors.

Richard knew there were ancient books on magic in the library to be found up in this area. It was only one of a number of libraries reserved for the Lord Rahl. Some were in this section, some in other restricted areas. While some were considerably larger, this one was special in other ways.

He suspected that this particular library was the reason his ancestors hadn't wanted anyone else having unfettered access to this area of the palace. That, and they hadn't wanted just anyone nosing around. Considering the dangerous nature of the books in that library, Richard knew that he also had to keep access restricted.

While ungifted people wouldn't be able to understand those books or make use of them, if stolen they would bring a high price from the right people. Also, anyone gifted with even modest ability, should they try using those tomes, could accidentally invoke dangerous spells without realizing what they were doing.

Richard idly wondered if any of the spells in those ancient books could be useful to him in the present situation. He knew they contained powerful magic, but the problem was, he didn't know how to use much of it.

Having grown up in a place without magic he'd had no training in the use of his gift. But such training would have been of no real value. Because he had been gifted as a war wizard, his powers worked differently than in anyone else and training would have been of no help to him. Unlike other gifted people, his gift as a war wizard was linked inextricably to anger. Anger was a necessary tool in combat, and thus essential in a war wizard.

Still, since leaving the Hartland woods, he had learned a lot about magic, and he knew the danger of those books. He had read many of them, as well as many other books of magic in other libraries both at the People's Palace, and in other places. At times, such books had proved useful to him. They had explained much, and unlocked many secrets.

On the way to the library, they had picked up a fair number of men of the First File. With the new danger from the goddess and her kind, the officers wanted to make sure Richard and Kahlan were always well protected. Although it was at times awkward to be surrounded by soldiers, Richard, a loner by nature, knew it was necessary. While half a dozen Mord-Sith in red leather trailed right behind, one group of armed men checked the way ahead as another group marched along in the rear. Richard felt a bit like a prized pig being taken to a fair.

He understood that as the Lord Rahl he didn't have the right to needlessly put himself in harm's way, so he had grown somewhat used to being constantly protected. He was at least gratified to have Kahlan under that protection as well. As a Confessor, she had grown up with others rightly concerned about her safety, so it wasn't odd to her.

The corridor they were in had a thick carpet with a pattern of leaves in various shades of browns. The carpeting and sizable wall hangings gave the corridor a muted, calm feel. The carpet also quieted all the footsteps, which in turn only served to highlight the jangle of weapons and chain mail.

Along the way there were graceful wooden tables and comfortable chairs with studded metalwork on them. Most of the tables held vases, many with flowers. Some of the colorful blown-glass vases were quite elaborate and were there simply for their own beauty. Paintings along the walls showed forest scenes, lakes, and mountains. They reminded Richard of how much he missed being alone in the quiet of his woods. He missed those peaceful times when there was no one, and nothing, trying to kill everyone in the world.

It was a troubling concept to grasp, and it occurred to him that the calm beauty of the restricted areas was a way for the Lord Rahl to have his mind quieted in order for him to ponder unfathomable threats to the world.

It was amazing that in such a short time, they had gone from lower levels with horrific sights, to such a beautiful and peaceful area. All in the same palace.

14

As they quickly made their way down the elegant corridor, Richard spotted the group of people assembled in the distance. Most were sitting on the ugly orange-striped chairs outside the library. There was a group of soldiers there as well, to watch over the guests in the restricted area.

As they got close enough for the group to see that it was Lord Rahl approaching, in his war-wizard outfit, gold cape and all, along with the Mother Confessor in her white dress, the guests all shot to their feet.

When Richard and his group were close enough, all the people, except the soldiers, went on to a knee, bowing forward, as was the old tradition when meeting the Mother Confessor.

Richard saw a number of those people trembling.
He didn't know if it was out of fear of him, or
the Mother Confessor. He remembered after
he had first met Kahlan, when they crossed the
boundary into the Midlands, he saw people
of every kind, including kings and queens, fall
to their knees before Kahlan. Many of those,
too, had trembled. Many people believed that a
Confessor could steal their minds if she chose.
In a way, that was true, but not in the way many
people feared.

Kahlan came to a halt before the bowed,
silent people.

"Rise, my children."

Everyone returned to their feet, but none of
them looked any more at ease. None of them
would look up into either Richard's or Kahlan's
eyes.

"I want to thank you all for coming," Richard
said in as friendly a tone as he could muster.
Below the surface he was boiling with rage over
the murders of so many people down in the dark
recesses of the palace, but he knew he couldn't
show that anger to these people. "It's an honor
for me to finally get the chance to meet the
gifted living here at the People's Palace."

One woman, with frizzy faded brown hair and in a plain, straight tan dress with no belt, held up a hand. When Richard nodded to her, she spoke in a meek voice.

"I am gifted, Lord Rahl." Her other hand settled on the shoulder of a girl with her back up against the woman. "But my daughter, Dori, is not. Also, we don't live here. We are merely visitors to the palace, come to watch the audiences you granted in the great hall the other day."

Richard supposed she wanted to make that clear just in case the Lord Rahl suddenly took on the disposition of Richard's father and decided to imprison the gifted who lived at the palace, or at least restrict their lives in some way.

Richard smiled at the woman. "I'm sure your daughter is no less of a handful, and no less of a joy, for being ungifted. The Mother Confessor and I are grateful that you came to visit the People's Palace."

That brought a smile to the woman. The smile looked to have surprised her at its unexpected arrival, causing her to blush.

The daughter, Dori, seemed to be even more shy than her mother. She wore a faded blue dress dotted with little white flowers and cinched at the waist by a thin woven cord belt tied at her hip. Her straight brown hair, parted in the middle, hung just short of her bony shoulders. She seemed too fearful to be able to bring herself to look up at the Lord Rahl towering above her. Richard studied her a moment as she turned her head, looking away to the side to avoid eye contact.

He finally clasped his hands behind his back as he strolled before the rest of the group, getting a good look at them all, and they at him. There were two older men with white hair and beards, one very old woman with short, wavy white hair, half a dozen young men and women still in their teens, and all the rest in a variety of years in between.

"You all are gifted in some way?" Richard asked.

Many of their eyes shifted to the half-dozen Mord-Sith standing off behind him before looking back and nodding, some slowly, some enthusiastically. Some even smiled with confident pride.

"Good. I'm truly honored to finally have the chance to meet all of you." He smiled again.

"Perhaps some of you have known your gift as far back as you can remember. I was shocked, myself, when I first learned that I'm gifted."

That brought broader smiles to most of them and seemed to at least put others at ease to know he was human.

"Are there any among you who have been formally trained in the use of your gift?"

One of the older men, and three of the middle-aged women, lifted a hand.

"Can you tell me how?" Richard asked, pointing at the man.

He cleared his throat. "I was trained in prophecy, Lord Rahl. By an uncle who has long since passed away," he hastened to add.

"Are you gifted in any other way?"

The man winced a little, as if afraid to disappoint Richard. "No, Lord Rahl. Just with prophecy, I'm afraid."

"Are there any others among you who are gifted in prophecy?"

Everyone shook their heads. Richard turned back to the older man.

"And have you had any prophecy recently?"

He looked abashed. "I used to be visited by prophecy regularly, Lord Rahl, but I'm afraid that since the end of the war, I've no longer had any prophecies."

Richard didn't want to tell the man that he had ended prophecy, so instead he offered a smile. "All right, thank you for coming. If prophecy returns to you, please be sure to send word to me and perhaps I will call on you again, but that's all that I need for now." Richard held a hand out toward nearby stairs that led down to the public area. "Sorry to have asked you up here for nothing."

As the man thanked Richard and dipped a bow, Shale came up behind Richard to speak in a confidential tone.

"Lord Rahl, I think I can be of assistance."

"What do you mean?"

"I can very easily test each of these people for the scope of their ability and the specific talents of each. I believe it would make things go much faster, but more importantly we would get a true accounting of their actual ability, untainted by exaggerated boasting or imagined abilities."

"That makes sense. I've seen people before who thought they were gifted when they really weren't." He turned back to the waiting group. "Shale, here, is a talented sorceress. She is going to assist me by testing each of you to see if you have a specific ability I'm looking for."

Richard didn't really have a specific ability he was looking for, as he had already found exactly what he sought.

But he was interested in knowing if anyone gifted with considerable power was among the group. That kind of person would worry the Golden Goddess and might possibly be useful.

Shale started in the back and worked her way among the group. As she approached each person, she smiled and told them to simply relax. She then placed a hand to each side of their head, in much the same way a mother might hold the face of a beloved child. She tested Dori's mother, the woman who was visiting, last. Dori looked down and away, as if too shy to watch a sorceress at her craft.

Shale finally returned, taking Richard's arm on the way past and leading him back a number of paces, out of earshot of the group. Kahlan went with them, wanting to know what Shale had discovered.

"Well?" Richard finally asked when they came to a stop. "What did you learn?"

Shale looked disappointed. "There are a variety of talents among these people. One man started training in the craft of wizardry. His gift is weak and not adequate enough that it could be developed into much of anything. A few of the women have a talent for sorcery, but it is a bit hard to call it a 'talent.' It's more like a shallow hint. A number of them have minor healing ability. Some have a variety of other talents, but those talents are only latent, at best, and profoundly weak."

"Who is the strongest among them?" Kahlan asked. "Who has the most power?"

Shale briefly cast a glance back over her shoulder before turning a frown on her and Richard.

"In all honesty, I don't think that the whole lot of them have enough combined power to be able to light a candle."

"Really?" Richard was mildly disappointed, because he had been hoping, along with his true interest for calling them all together, to maybe find among them some who were gifted enough to possibly help defend them. "None of them have even a modest amount of gift?"

Shale shook her head regretfully. "I'm afraid not, Lord Rahl. I think the strongest healer among them might have the power to pull out a splinter, but that's about it. Many of them are quite proud of their gift, but not for sound reason."

Kahlan's attention was focused on Richard. "You don't look very discouraged."

Richard showed her a brief smile. "I'm not. I found what I was looking for."

Before she could ask what he had been looking for, he returned to the group. Shale and Kahlan followed, Shale looking puzzled, Kahlan with a look of growing concern.

Kahlan leaned in close from behind. "Richard, are you having one of your crazy ideas?"

"He gets crazy ideas?" Shale asked in a whisper.

"You don't know the half of it," Kahlan whispered back. "Trust me on this one."

Richard ignored them both and instead paused to take hold of Vika's arm and pull her close. He tipped his head down toward her and spoke with quiet meaning. "I want you to look after Dori's mother for me."

Vika understood the look and so didn't question the order. Her expression hardened. "Not a problem, Lord Rahl. I will take care of it."

Richard returned to stand before the group, hands again casually clasped behind his back. "I would like to thank you all for coming. We have everything we needed to know. We have learned that your abilities are all quite special. For now, you may go back to what you were doing. If we discover that we have need of your unique talents, we will contact you."

He held an arm out, indicating the stairway not far down the corridor, which was guarded by four soldiers with pikes.

Before the mother and daughter could leave with the rest of the group, Richard held a hand up to signal the woman to remain behind.

She frowned. "Yes, Lord Rahl?"

"Actually," Richard said, "I would like to speak to your daughter, Dori."

Dori's head was bowed, her gaze cast down at the floor; she was too afraid to look up at the big, scary Lord Rahl.

Richard went to one knee and leaned close. He put a finger under her chin to lift her face up toward him. She turned her eyes away, still afraid to meet his gaze.

"What is it you want?" she asked in a small voice.

"I would like to surrender," Richard said in a quiet, confidential tone that only she could hear.

The girl's eyes suddenly looked up at him from under her brow, and then she slowly smiled in a way that no innocent little girl ever could.

15

Vika stepped in front of the little girl's mother as she started to reach for her daughter. Vika lifted her Agiel and, with the weapon pointed toward the mother, began backing her away.

"What a very, very wise decision," the girl said in a low, husky voice. It was a voice that sounded as if it could crush bone.

Without looking back, Richard lifted a finger behind himself when he sensed Kahlan starting to come forward. At his warning, she stopped in her tracks.

"Please"—Richard rose and held out his hand in invitation—"let's go in here where we can talk in private."

Richard didn't wait for an answer or explain

to the others. He strode to the room and opened the double glass doors without slowing, one hand on each handle as he swept into the room, his cape billowing out behind him. The girl glided in after him, glancing over to give Kahlan a murderous look on her way past. Once she was in the room, Richard turned and closed the doors. He twisted the lock so that no one else could enter. With the doors secure, he pulled the thick drapes over them. They had squares of special glass that people couldn't actually see through, but light could still come in. The drapes prevented that.

Dori, her back straight, slowly strolled around the center of the room, gazing at the walls of books, looking up and around, taking in everything as if viewing it from an alien world.

As large as the room was, it was actually one of the smaller libraries in the palace. All the walls except the one at the end with the glass were lined with shelves reaching up to a high, beamed ceiling. A brass rail with a ladder hooked to it ran past shelf after shelf packed tight with books of every size.

The tooled leather covers on some of the books looked timeworn. Even with their great age, it was easy to see the care with which they had been made to denote their importance. Richard knew, though, that the most dangerous volumes in the library looked simple and not at all important, and that the most important-looking books, crafted with great care and skill, were not actually all that special. It was a simple method the wizards of old used to throw off would-be thieves and those who had no business looking for dangerous spells. It was something, among a great many other things, that Zedd, his grandfather, had taught him.

Each side of the long room had three rows of freestanding bookcases. Some of the cases held enormous, oversize volumes. Some of the covers and spines of those had titles in gold foil. One of the cases had locked glass doors covering the entire face of it, further restricting access to the books it contained in a room that was already highly restricted.

The glass doors weren't simply locked. Richard knew that the books behind those glass doors were some of the most dangerous of the books in the library, books so dangerous that the wizards of the time when the library had been created did not want to trust the simple trick of making those books look unimportant. Those glass doors were sealed with spells that required considerable skill and Subtractive Magic to open.

Richard knew that many of the most dangerous books, those on the shelves and those behind locked glass doors, spoke of him. They called him by many different names. They spoke of him centuries before he had even been born. They expressed grave warnings, and profound hopes.

On the distant side of the room to Richard's left, beyond the rows of bookcases, there was a sitting area with three comfortable-looking chairs. Except that he couldn't imagine anyone using them, because they had the same ugly orange stripes as the chairs in the sitting area outside the library. Richard knew the true purpose of the ugly orange stripes.

In the center of the room, between the rows of bookcases to each side, stood a long, heavy oak table with massive, turned wooden legs. A few wooden chairs sat at random angles around it, as if the people using them had just gotten up for a moment, but never came back. Richard had been one of those people.

A number of simple, unimportant-looking books lay open on the table. Richard was the one, quite a while back, who had left those books there. A few small stacks of books on the table were ones he had collected from the shelves and left there in case he needed to come back to search them for things that could help him. The whole library looked like a cozy, inviting place to read. But Richard knew that, like some others, this room was more than simply a library, and it was anything but cozy.

As Dori gazed about the room, he went to the end of the far wall on his right and pulled the heavy drapes across the tall windows made up of squares of thick, clouded glass. It was a very special type of glass that only the most knowledgeable wizards in an age long past knew how to make. It took not only Additive Magic to create such spiraled glass, but Subtractive as well, to say nothing of special knowledge and arcane skills.

"What are you doing?" Dori asked. She sounded annoyed and impatient.

"Just hoping to make you comfortable," Richard said over his shoulder as he made sure the drapes were light-tight.

When satisfied, he blew out the flame on one of the nearby reflector lamps. He smiled at her.

"I know how you prefer the dark."

"I have spent time with that woman, the mother of this body. She has magic," Dori added with growling distaste. "Magic is not the incomprehensible mystery I thought at first. I have observed the woman and it is not so strong a thing, this magic your kind has."

"No," Richard agreed with a sigh. "I suppose not."

He blew out the flame of another lamp on his way by. With the heavy drapes drawn over the windows and doors, only two lamps, one at either end of the room, were left to light the grand library. They were woefully inadequate for the task and left the middle of the room in deep shadows. Dori smiled her approval. Richard had to be careful not to run into the rows of bookcases.

"What are the terms for my surrender?" he asked as he returned to the center of the room.

"Terrrrms?" she rasped. "No terrrrms." The very word was obviously distasteful to her. "Surrender is unconditional. In return for saving me the trouble of having to hunt you down and kill you, I will grant you the indulgence of a quick death. It will be terrifyingly painful, of course, but quick. That is your reward for surrendering. That, and the knowledge that you will not have to witness what is to come for the rest of your world. You should be groveling at my feet in gratitude for sparing you that."

"What about the Mother Confessor?"

Dori frowned her displeasure. "She did not offer to surrender. Unlike you, she still resists the inevitable. She will again feel our claws, but this time, as she screams her lungs out, she will also feel our teeth as they rip her face from her skull. We will suck out her eyes and brains and gorge on her flesh. We will smear her blood on ourselves for the pleasure of the warm, wet, greasy feel of it."

Richard desperately wanted to draw his sword. Its magic was screaming for release. He denied that magic its urgent need. He controlled his own rage, as the Sisters of the Light had for so long sought to teach him. As he smiled at the little girl, it occurred to him that the Sisters would be proud of how far he had come.

What they wouldn't have understood, though,

was how he was able to turn that fury inward. Richard blew out one of the two remaining lamps by the ugly orange chairs and then returned to the center of the room. In the murky light of the one remaining lamp off in the distance behind him, he could barely see Dori at the opposite end of the long table.

"Who are you, exactly?" Richard asked across the length of the heavy table. "It seems I should be allowed to know who you are, since I have agreed to surrender."

"I am the Golden Goddess."

Richard shrugged. "Well, I know that much. What I mean is"—he leaned in—"who are you? What are you?"

Dori effortlessly sprang up onto the top of the other end of the heavy oak table like something out of a nightmare. She slowly walked down the length of the table toward him, her heels clicking with each measured step, a predator locked on to its prey.

"I am the bringer of the tide of my kind," she said in a low, guttural growl. "A coming tide that will wash over your kind, wash over your world, and drown you all." She came to a halt above him at his end of the table. She glared down at him. "I am the Golden Goddess, the bringer of that tide."

In the dead silence, with shadows all around her, she slowly lifted both arms out at her sides and opened her fingers, palms up, summoning that tide forth.

First one began to appear, then another; then the whole room started coming alive with movement. It was just as Kahlan had described it, like scribbles in the air, dizzyingly fast lines upon swirling lines, faster and faster, arcing, looping, tracing through the air, indications of their shape and mass and size. Because it was impossible to make it all fit any notion of what was real, what was solid, what existed, and what didn't, it was a disorienting sight.

At least it was until those scribbly lines began to thicken, as if they were now being drawn in gooey, muddy water. Those thickening lines began to fuse together, revealing their true forms, until they finally materialized in the gloom all around him. The whole process took only seconds, but in those few seconds, the whole world seemed to change as it suddenly came alive with creatures more terrifying than anything he could have imagined.

"My children," Dori said in a low, menacing snarl as she held out her arms, this time in introduction. "They have come for you."

All around, more and more of those scribbles in midair were coalescing into dark, wet shapes, tall, massive, and muscular. They stood on two legs, hunched a little. He could just make out the claws at the ends of powerful arms. Steam or vapor of some kind rose from the black, glistening bodies. Globs of gelatinous material slid down off their lumpy, amphibious-like skin, dripping from the creatures to splash on the floor.

"Who are you?" Richard asked in a whisper as more and more of the creatures were continually materializing in the shadows all around, each one scribbles at first, then becoming its full form, until they packed the room with their tall, black, steaming, dripping shapes.

When their wide mouths opened and their thin lips drew back in a kind of snarl, Richard could see their long, sharp, pointed teeth. Those sharp white teeth stood out against the wet, black bodies. Slime drew out in thin strands between the top and bottom teeth as they opened their mouths wider, hissing with threat.

"Who are you?" Richard asked Dori again,

appalled at what he was seeing all around him. "I mean, who are your kind? What are you? What are you called?"

"We are the Gleeeee," she said, dragging the name out in a guttural growl that was bone-chilling.

Hundreds of them, it seemed, surrounded him, packed into every available space in the library, some even crouched atop the rows of bookcases, all leaning in toward him. The steam rising from their wet bodies collected like a cloud near the ceiling. Their lumpy black skin shimmered in the shadowy light. Their teeth clacked as they snapped their jaws at him.

"The Glee," Richard repeated.

"Yessss," she said as she grinned with evil intent.

"But how are you able to be in the body of this girl? How do the Glee travel from your world to ours?"

"I am able to put my mind into this body."

Richard frowned. "But how?"

"Because I am the one who presently serves as the Golden Goddess, my mind is able to go to those places where I send the Gleeeee. I am able to enter the mind of another. I am now in this pathetic, weak, skin creature."

Richard gestured up at all the menacing creatures behind her. "And how are your kind able to come here, to our world?"

"We come." Dori cocked her head. "We collect other worlds. It is what we do."

Richard realized that, for whatever reason, he wasn't going to be able to get any better explanation out of her, possibly because she didn't know how they did it, only that they did. He guessed that maybe it was something like someone asking him how he breathed, how he walked, and how he was able to talk. Like her, he just knew that he did.

He gazed around at the hundreds of creatures packed into the library, their wet bodies sliding against one another as they vied for a better position, trying to get closer to their prey.

"Why did you need to bring so many just to kill me?"

"Because I wanted the Gleeeee to see that your magic is not to be feared so they can tell others. With caution about magic dispelled, we will become a tide that will wash over your world. I am the Golden Goddess. I am the bringer of that tide."

16

"What do you suppose he is doing in there?" Shale asked as she paused to gaze nervously at the double doors before turning her attention back to Kahlan.

The woman's pacing was starting to get on Kahlan's nerves. She knew that something was terribly wrong, and her heart already hammered in dread. Richard had wanted to see all the gifted in the palace, and when they proved to have very little useful power, Kahlan had thought he would be disappointed, but he wasn't.

It was obvious to her now that he'd had some kind of plan when he called all those gifted people up to the library area. Kahlan didn't know what that plan had been or what it was he had been looking for, but she did know that it had brought him what he had been seeking. Kahlan worried what his real reason could have been for wanting to see all the gifted. More worrisome, though, was what he could have really been looking for, and what he had found.

He was the Seeker, of course, and Kahlan had seen him do such inexplicable things before. Kahlan knew Richard, and she knew that he was focused on something. Something dangerous. Something so dangerous that he hadn't told her what he was really doing or what it was about.

Kahlan slowly shook her head as Shale stood over her, waiting for an answer. "If I know Richard, and I do, he has gotten some crazy idea into his head."

"Crazy idea?" Shale was clearly agitated by the answer and considered it unsatisfactory. "You said that before. What kind of crazy idea?"

"Lord Rahl gets crazy ideas sometimes," Berdine said, coming to Kahlan's rescue.

Shale paused in her pacing to stare incredulously at the Mord-Sith.

"How do you know that?"

"I know because I am Lord Rahl's favorite," Berdine explained with a grin.

Whereas the others were tall, muscular,

and blond, Berdine had wavy brown hair, also pulled back into a single braid. She was shorter than the others, too, with a curvier, solid build. While she looked different from the other Mord-Sith, and had a rather flippant nature, she was no less devoted or deadly.

Shale blinked at the woman. "His favorite?"

"He doesn't have favorites," Kahlan absently reminded her as she stared again at the double doors. "He's told you many times, Berdine, that he loves you all equally."

Berdine beamed as she nodded. "I know. But he loves me more equally."

Kahlan could only shake her head. She didn't feel like indulging Berdine's nonsense. Kahlan knew that Berdine sometimes turned to the distraction of such seemingly inane banter when she was worried for Richard.

Kahlan was worried for him, too. She thought again about how she had heard Richard lock the latch on the double doors. Was he worried about someone interrupting them? Or did he want to lock Dori in for some crazy reason?

"What is she talking about?" Shale complained. Kahlan had learned over the years that sorceresses tended to complain a lot. It was part of their nature. An annoying part. "What does she mean about Richard getting crazy ideas?"

Kahlan, sitting on the front edge of one of the ugly orange chairs, hands in her lap, her back straight, finally looked up at Shale when she came insistently closer, expecting an answer.

Kahlan lifted a hand in a vague gesture. "Richard sometimes has crazy ideas. At least, they always seem crazy to us at the time, but they're not crazy to Richard. He is always running odd little bits of information and strange calculations through his head that none of us could possibly know about or understand and so the things he says or does can seem . . . crazy."

"That's the truth," Cassia chimed in. "I haven't known him as long as some of the others, but I certainly have seen him get crazy ideas."

A few of the other Mord-Sith nodded that they, too, were all too familiar with Richard's crazy ideas.

"It isn't just that Lord Rahl gets crazy ideas," Nyda explained. "The man *is* crazy. Stone-cold crazy. That's why he has crazy ideas. That's why he needs all of us to protect him."

Shale looked appalled. "You mean he does that a lot?" she asked as she leaned down toward Kahlan. "Get these crazy ideas?"

Kahlan glanced to the doors again before answering the sorceress. "I don't know. Sometimes he just does. A lot of times it's simply hard to imagine what he's thinking. He doesn't always have the time or patience to explain things. I don't know how to explain the ideas he gets in his head."

"That's because they're crazy," Berdine offered, helpfully.

Kahlan ignored her. "Sometimes when we all think we know exactly what we must do, then he suddenly does the opposite. Or he comes up with something out of the blue that no one expected or understands. Sometimes he does things as the Seeker that he knows he has to do, and we just don't know his reasoning, so it seems crazy to us, that's all."

"Like what?" Shale pressed.

Kahlan got up from the chair and went to the doors. She leaned close, putting an ear almost against the glass for a moment. She didn't hear anything. As she returned to Shale and Berdine she hooked a long strand of hair behind an ear.

Kahlan gave the sorceress a look. "Like deciding that to save the world he must end prophecy. Does that sound normal to you?"

Shale made a face. "No. I've never seen him do anything I would call crazy, but now that you mention it, that most definitely would have sounded crazy to me." She shook her head. "I have to say, it still does."

"Well," Kahlan said, gesturing at the locked doors, "now you have seen him do something else that seems a bit crazy."

Shale conceded with a sigh.

17

Kahlan glanced over at Vika, a ways down the corridor. The Mord-Sith had backed the girl's mother off quite a distance. The woman was wringing her hands in worry, peeking around Vika from time to time, trying to see what was happening with her daughter. Kahlan worried about that, too.

A few dozen men of the First File stood guard farther down to each direction of the corridor, well beyond the sitting area outside the library. The upper level of the palace was generally quite elegant. Most of it was calming and hushed. All the decorations and beautiful art contributed to that sense of tranquility. It seemed rather odd to her, considering the types of men who had been the Lord Rahl throughout history. In recent centuries, they had been a long string of tyrants, and the world was never calm and tranquil under their rule.

The one thing that didn't fit with all the tasteful areas of the upper corridor was the orange-striped chairs in the sitting area outside this particular library. They were terribly uncomfortable to lean back in and were so ugly that Kahlan didn't really like to sit on them.

"Why do you think they would have put chairs like this in such a beautiful corridor?" she said out loud to no one in particular.

Shale frowned at the question and then looked around at the chairs. "What's wrong with them?"

"What's wrong with them? They're grotesque."

Kahlan's feet hurt from standing, so, as much as she didn't like the chairs, she sat down again on the very front edge of one.

Berdine patted a hand in a familiar manner on the back of one of the chairs. "Richard's father, Darken Rahl, never liked coming up here because he didn't like these chairs, either."

Kahlan stared openly at the Mord-Sith. "Then why in the world didn't he order them changed? He routinely ordered the execution of countless innocent people. He delighted in throwing people from different lands into slavery and indentured servitude. He ruined lives across D'Hara and then the Midlands without a second thought. He ruled with an iron fist.

"So why, if he didn't like these chairs, wouldn't he order them removed, burned, and replaced with something else?"

Berdine raised her eyebrows, as if it were a silly question. "Because they have to be here." The way she said it made it sound obvious.

Kahlan pressed the middle finger and thumb of one hand to opposite temples in an effort to calm herself. She had a headache from thinking about the helpless terror of all those poor, innocent people who had been slaughtered down in the lower reaches of the palace. The tension of this new threat was getting to her. She knew that her pregnancy had something to do with it. She was in a constant state of worry for the two babies growing inside her.

She took a deep breath before asking, "Why do these chairs have to be here?"

"Because they have ugly magic."

"What?" Kahlan made a face at the woman.

"Ugly magic? These chairs have ugly magic? What in the world kind of magic is ugly magic?"

"Well," she said, gesturing to the closed doors, "that room is dangerous. It's a repository, a containment field, for very dangerous spells. Darken Rahl rarely went in there himself. I'm pretty sure he was afraid of that room, although he never admitted as much."

"What does that have to do with these ugly chairs?"

Berdine shrugged. "There are inviting places everywhere." She gestured back down the corridor one way and then the other. "There are many comfortable, beautiful places outside other libraries to sit. You can sit and relax almost anywhere you like up on this level."

"Well then," Kahlan said with exaggerated patience, "who would want to sit here in these uncomfortable, ugly, orange-striped chairs?"

Berdine smiled. "Exactly."

Shale blinked. "You mean, these chairs are—"

"You mean, they're meant to discourage people from lingering here in front of that dangerous room," Kahlan said, suddenly understanding.

Berdine nodded with a smile that Kahlan

finally caught on. "One time," she confided in both Kahlan and Shale, looking back and forth between them as if revealing a secret, "Darken Rahl said that a person would have to be crazy to use the room with the orange-striped chairs."

"Crazy . . ." Kahlan glanced to the double doors. "Crazy, like Richard."

Berdine confirmed it with a single nod of satisfaction. "You see? Ugly magic."

Kahlan stood to gesture toward the doors. "Does Richard know that this room is dangerous?"

Berdine snorted a laugh. "Are you kidding? Of course he knows. Back when Lord Rahl— your Lord Rahl, not Darken Rahl, not that Lord Rahl—asked me to help him do research on things he desperately needed to find out, he asked me to go to all the libraries throughout the palace to search the reference works referring to specific things he needed."

Kahlan frowned. "So?"

Berdine leaned in again, lowering her voice as if someone might overhear, even though there was no one other than Shale and Kahlan within earshot.

"So, when Lord Rahl asked me to search the

reference books in all the libraries, he told me, 'Except the one with the orange-striped chairs. I don't want you going in that room—not for any reason. I will search that library myself.' That's how I know that he knew the place is dangerous. Of course, I knew it was dangerous before, because of Darken Rahl."

Just then an onslaught of piercing shrieks erupted. Along with everyone else, Kahlan looked toward the doors. It sounded like the shrieks of demons.

Then came a collective howl so horrifying that it made Kahlan flinch in fright. The horrible screech from beyond the doors echoed through the corridor. Everyone—the soldiers, the Mord-Sith, Shale, and Kahlan—all turned to gape at the library. The sound made the hair on Kahlan's arms and neck stand on end.

18

The hundreds of bloodcurdling shrieks joined into one collective howl that felt as if it tore the very fibers of Kahlan's nerves. Her heart pounded out of control in her chest. She knew that the slaughtered people down below had heard those same shrieks as they were being ripped apart. She knew because she had heard one of those horrifying shrieks when she had been attacked, one claw pierced into her side to hold her while the other claw ripped down through the muscles of her arm.

The wail of it made her freshly healed claw wounds throb in sudden pain. Kahlan covered her ears, trying to shut out the horrifying sound. Tears sprang to her eyes from the bone-tingling terror for her husband beyond those doors.

Then, the whole palace shook with a sudden jolt that nearly took them all from their feet.

The powerful shock that rocked the palace made Shale gasp. The Mord-Sith spread their feet and went into a crouch to keep their balance. Kahlan grabbed one of the high-backed orange-striped chairs for support. Some of the others fell over.

She saw the doors to the library shudder in their frame, but they held, and not even the glass broke from the violent jolt that had come from inside that room. It was, after all, a containment field, so she would have expected the doors to hold. That brutal jolt to the palace brought an abrupt end to the needful, murderous howls.

In one instant, Kahlan had to cover her ears, and in the next instant, everything went dead quiet. She lowered her hands from her ears.

"Earthquake?" Shale asked in the sudden silence.

Kahlan shook her head. "I don't think so. It was just one big jolt. I'm not sure, but I think earthquakes shake more. This was more like an explosion. And besides, it came from in there, not underfoot."

Shale looked confused. "But there was no

sound of an explosion. How could there be no sound?"

"Outside a containment field you wouldn't necessarily hear the explosive release of profoundly violent magic, but you couldn't help but to feel it."

Shale gave one cynical shake of her head. "I've never heard of a containment field before. But I guess it's not the kind of thing to be found in the Northern Waste."

Kahlan hurried to the room and pounded a fist on the door. She didn't care if he was doing something and wanted to be left alone. That wish had suddenly been nullified as far as she was concerned.

"Richard!" When there was no answer, she pounded again. "Richard! Are you all right? What's going on?"

She stepped back when all of a sudden, the doors burst open. Thick black smoke billowed out and spread across the ceiling of the corridor. Men of the First File were already rushing to the scene from every direction. Glowing embers floated and whirled out with the sooty smoke.

Berdine and the other Mord-Sith ran toward the open doorway, followed closely by Shale.

With all the black smoke, it was hard to see inside the room. Kahlan held an arm out to stop the others. She didn't think it would be wise to blindly charge into the room.

"Richard!" Kahlan called into the darkness, fearing the worst.

"I'm here," he said in a quiet voice as he seemed to materialize out of the swirling, inky smoke and burning embers. Kahlan expected the smoke to smell acrid. It didn't. Not at all. Oddly, rather than smelling like anything burning she had ever smelled before, it smelled like nothing so much as a stagnant swamp.

"Dear spirits, what happened? What was that explosion or whatever it was?" Kahlan asked as she gripped his upper arm. "It shook the whole palace."

Before he could say anything, Shale leaned around him to look into the room as the smoke was beginning to thin and clear. "Where's Dori?"

Rather than answer, Richard gave her a forbidding look, then turned and disappeared back into the swirling smoke, the gold of his cape swallowed by the murky haze. As the haze started to clear, the room began brightening.

Apparently, Richard had opened the drapes over the windows.

Once there was enough light from those windows and coming in through the open double doors, Berdine, Nyda, Rikka, Vale, Cassia, and Vika pushed past Shale and then Kahlan to hurry into the room. Each of them had her Agiel in her fist. Ignoring the fetid smell from inside, Kahlan cautiously followed them in, with Shale right behind her.

The sight of the inside of the room was not at all what Kahlan had expected. She had expected nothing but a charred shell. Instead, it appeared mostly intact. The shelves she could see rising up all around into the smoke still hanging near the high ceiling looked relatively undamaged. The books were intact and all still on their shelves.

But it was clear that something in the room had been incinerated.

There were countless black splotches, as if countless clots of greasy soot had been hurled against the walls, the books, the shelves. There were splashes of that dark, grimy substance everywhere, on nearly everything. Hundreds of those masses had impacted against the walls of books all around, leaving them looking like hundreds of clusters of dirty, greasy ash had been blasted against them. All of those sprays of soot lumped up in the center of each splash, with a starlike pattern thrown out from that center. Wisps of smoke still floated up from each of those clots. The floor was covered with the still-smoking substance. It was so deep that Kahlan's shoes sank into it. As the smoke gradually thinned out, she could see the same kind of grimy splatters all over the ceiling.

Kahlan couldn't imagine what had made such an incredible mess.

"What in the world . . . " Shale whispered as she stared up at the dark disorder all around the room. She turned and frowned at Richard. "Where is Dori? The little girl you came in here with. Where is she?"

Richard fixed the sorceress in his raptor gaze a moment, and then went to the end of the table. There was a small pile of ash on the end of the table, but this particular pile wasn't black. It was gray.

Richard put a hand under the edge of the table and with his other hand wiped the ash off the table and into his upturned palm.

He took it to the sorceress. "Hold out your hands."

Shale regarded him suspiciously. "Why?"

The muscles in Richard's jaw flexed. "Hold out your hands."

Reluctantly, Shale finally did as he asked, lifting her hands, holding them together, palms up. Richard let the ash slowly pour into her hands.

"This is what is left of Dori," he said in a low, menacing tone. "Since you are such an advocate of bringing innocent children into a world in the middle of this terrible threat, where they will be helpless, where they will be hunted, where they will be subjected to horrors with no way to defend themselves, I want you to take the remains of this child to her mother, and tell her that her precious daughter was possessed by an evil force and died because of it."

Shale looked horrified. "Lord Rahl, I don't think I can—"

"Do it!" Richard yelled right into her face. "You think this world is safe for children and wanted Kahlan and me to have children despite the monsters that hunt us. This is the kind of thing that would await them. You take this child's remains to her mother, and you tell her that we are sorry but none of us could protect her daughter from evil—just like none of us could protect Kahlan and my children from this evil."

Kahlan wanted to tell him that it wasn't Shale's fault, but at the sight of Richard's anger over the death of a child, she was paralyzed. She was going to have to tell him sooner or later, but she wanted it to be a joyful announcement of her pregnancy. She didn't want to have such wonderful news come out when something had just happened that had Richard in a rage, or when someone else's child had just died.

Worse, apparently died at Richard's hands.

Shale, still standing with her hands out, holding the pile of ashes, swallowed. Seeing the look in his eyes, she finally nodded in resignation.

As Shale left to do his bidding, Kahlan threw her arms around Richard, hugging him close. She could feel him trembling. She didn't know if it was in rage, or from what had just happened in this room.

She wanted to tell him that everything was all right, now, but she knew it wasn't. Whatever had happened was only a small part of a much larger menace, and it had involved a child losing her life. At a loss for words, Kahlan simply hugged him.

"I'm sorry," Richard whispered in her ear. "I'm so sorry. I do want to have children one day. I just can't imagine bringing them into a world with what I have just seen."

19

Kahlan wanted to know what had happened—what he had just seen—but she didn't want to press him for answers right then. Richard would tell her in his own way, in his own time. For the moment, she simply put her head against his shoulder and her arms around his waist.

By the time Shale returned with Vika, Kahlan had come to realize that Richard's trembling was anger. He had come out of the library room shaking in rage and that rage was still charging his muscles with tension. Worse, he hadn't even drawn his sword and called forth its fury. It was purely his anger.

"I did as you asked, Lord Rahl." Shale's face had lost some of its color.

Richard nodded. "Thank you. I don't imagine Dori's mother took the news well."

"No, she did not," Shale admitted. "But she did tell me something I think you should know. When I told her what you said, that her daughter had been possessed by evil and died because of it, she didn't act surprised. She cried at the loss, of course, but then told me that Dori had been acting strange ever since arriving at the palace."

"Strange how?" he asked.

"Cold and distant. She said that was unlike Dori and she began to fear that her daughter had been possessed by something depraved. That was the word she used, 'depraved.'"

Richard stared off into distant thoughts for a moment. "I have seen too many mothers lose their children. With the great war finally over, I thought I had seen the last of it. But now I know otherwise. We have only seen the beginning of it."

"A mother feeling that something was off about her daughter is understandable," Shale said, apparently trying to distract him from grim thoughts. "A mother would know. But, how did you?"

Richard let out a sigh. "She wouldn't look at me."

Shale looked skeptical. "Children usually are too shy to look at strangers, especially an authority figure. Being shy is not exactly unusual, especially not when meeting a frightening person like the Lord Rahl."

"I realize that," Richard said, "but there was something about the way she avoided looking at me that wasn't quite natural." He thought about it a moment before going on.

"Remember when we questioned Nolo? He wouldn't look at me, either. The Golden Goddess used Nolo to demand that we surrender, and if we did she would in return offer us a quick death. Later Nolo told us that the Golden Goddess called me the shiny man because she found it painful to look at me because of my gift. I remembered the way he wouldn't look at me in the great hall the other day. That was the goddess not wanting to look at me."

"That's it?" Kahlan asked, throwing her hands up. "Just that she wouldn't look at you? Richard, that hardly seems enough to prove that the Golden Goddess was watching through Dori's eyes."

"Well," Richard admitted, "that, and what she did when I leaned down close and told her that I wanted to surrender."

"What?" Shale asked.

Richard nodded. "When told her that I wanted to surrender, she looked up at me and grinned."

Kahlan still wasn't entirely convinced that meant that Dori was acting on behalf of the Golden Goddess. "Children often smile at the strangest times. I've seen little kids smile at me as they were wetting their pants."

Richard looked over at her, shaking his head. "Not like this. This was as evil a smile as I've ever seen. Once I told her that I wanted to surrender and took her into the library, she dropped all pretense and there was no longer any question about it. The goddess was possessing Dori.

"I closed the drapes and blew out all but one lamp to make her more comfortable—to make the goddess more comfortable looking at me. The shy little girl was gone; there was only the contemptuous Golden Goddess."

"You mean she showed her true self because you told her you wanted to surrender?" Kahlan asked.

"That's right. She thought she had me where she wanted me—surrendering and ready to die. But the thing that was really making her confident was the mistake she made."

"What mistake?" Berdine blurted out, too curious to keep quiet at a lull in his story when he stared off into the memory.

Richard smiled at her eagerness. Berdine was an old friend, and the two of them had a special bond. Berdine was something of a scholar, and they had grown close when searching through books together for answers about things such as the omen machine.

Vika was Richard's personal bodyguard. She was muscular, strong-headed, and reacted instantly with profound violence to any threat to Richard. Berdine would also protect Richard with her life, but the two had known each other for a long time, and he really did love her, although not more than the others.

"The mistake the Golden Goddess made was in the choice of a host. I don't know how she can do it, and she wasn't able to tell me, but somehow, she invaded Dori's mind in much the same way as she had used Nolo. But this time she wormed her way in deeper and for longer."

"Why choose a little girl?" Kahlan asked. "Just to look less suspicious?"

Richard folded his arms. "No. She chose Dori because her mother was bringing her to the palace, where we are, but more importantly, because Dori's mother has the gift. The gift may not be strong in her, but the Golden Goddess didn't know that. The goddess is wary of magic, so she wanted to have time to observe the mother's magic and take the measure of it, thinking magic is magic—all magic is the same. So, she chose the daughter of a gifted person, a gifted person who was going to the palace where we live. She thought she had an additional stroke of luck when the mother was called up here to meet with me."

"Well, it actually was a stroke of luck," Shale said.

Richard shook his head. "Not exactly. I suspected that the goddess would want to get close to a gifted person, or even try to get in the mind of a gifted person. That's why I called all the gifted up here to meet with us.

"If she had invaded the mind of a gifted person, I wanted to give the goddess a chance to get close to me. I knew she very well might inadvertently make herself known by being afraid to look into my eyes. Dori was the one, though, who wouldn't look at me. When I leaned down and told her that I wanted to surrender, she took the bait—or at least, the goddess did. The reason I had invited all the gifted up to this place, besides suspecting the goddess might be among them, was that I hoped to get the goddess into a containment field if she was in one of them."

Shale slapped the palm of a hand to her forehead. "You mean you thought that you could kill the goddess?"

"I told you," Berdine said, "he gets crazy ideas."

"No, I didn't think I could kill her," he said in a mocking tone over his shoulder at Berdine. "And it wasn't a crazy idea. I was hoping to get more information out of her, maybe learn their weaknesses. Maybe find at least something we could use against them."

"So, you lied to her?" Shale asked, sounding as if that was somehow cheating.

Richard showed her a lopsided smile. "I sure did. I lied through my teeth. She bought it, too. The goddess is arrogant. She believes that she is so terrifying that I would be afraid, feel hopeless, and simply give up."

"All right. All well and good." Kahlan pointed impatiently. "But, exactly, what happened in there?"

20

Richard pulled in a deep breath. "Well, the Golden Goddess decided, because of being around Dori's mother, that magic wasn't really so dangerous after all. Since she doesn't understand magic, she didn't grasp that the mother's gift wasn't very strong, and assumed that because the mother had magic, and that her magic wasn't very dangerous, then my magic and magic in general weren't really anything to be worried about.

"As I had hoped, she wanted her kind to come and see that there was nothing to fear from us, so she summoned a horde of them into the room. Hundreds. She wanted them to see how weak magic actually is by letting them kill me and then tell others, so that her kind would no longer need to be cautious."

Kahlan leaned in, expectantly. "What did they look like?"

He looked into her eyes. "It was just like you described it—at first, anyway. They first appear as what you called a scribbly man. But that is only the initial phase as they are coming to our world, not what they really look like. It's simply some kind of transitional phase as they begin to materialize here. It went fully dark before that one that attacked you completed its transition into our world, so you never actually saw what they look like."

In slack-jawed attention, Berdine impatiently rolled her hand. "So, what do they look like once they finish appearing?"

Richard appraised all the eyes watching him. Kahlan could see that he was reluctant to tell them. After having been attacked by one, she wasn't sure she wanted to hear the terrifying reality that all of those dead people below had faced.

"Bigger than me," Richard said, holding his hand up high above his head to illustrate. "Muscular, long arms, each with those three claws, with almost black skin that . . . I don't know. They didn't have skin like us, and they didn't have scales. The best way I can describe it is that it reminded me of the skin of a newt, or salamander, or even a tadpole. They were wet and slimy-looking, with globs of gelatinous material that slid down off their lumpy, amphibious-like skin."

Berdine wrinkled her nose. "That's disgusting."

Richard nodded his agreement. "Some kind of steam or smoke rose up off of them as they became solid. I suspected that was somehow a consequence of traveling to our world."

Berdine hooked her first two fingers. "Do they have fangs? Like snakes?"

Richard shook his head. "No. They have long, sharp white teeth, all about the same, and a whole lot of them in a row across the top and the bottom jaw.

"I asked Dori what her kind was called. She said they were called the Glee. Except that when she said it, it came out like a long, croaking hiss. I can't pronounce it the way she did. But I can tell you, it ran goose bumps up my arms to hear her say it."

"So then when happened?" Kahlan asked when he fell silent, staring off into the memory of it.

He gave her a look with a smile, which she thought was a little odd.

"Then she told me that she was the Golden Goddess, the bringer of the tide that would wash over our world and drown us all. All of those creatures were packed into the room, gathered around, all leaning in toward me, all snapping their jaws full of those long, sharp teeth, all eager to tear into me once she gave them the word."

"And then what?" Berdine asked, impatiently rolling her hand yet again to urge him on when he paused.

"When she told me that she was the Golden Goddess, the bringer of the tide that would wash over us, I smiled at her, and asked if she knew who I was. Her eyes narrowed, and for the first time she looked uncertain."

Berdine leaned in. "What'd you tell her?"

"I said, 'I am the bringer of death.'"

Berdine laughed with excitement at that.

"And then what?" Kahlan asked.

"And then," Richard said in a quiet tone, "along with everything else alive in that room, I had to kill that child."

He paused for a moment before looking back at them and going on.

"I unleashed the full fury of that which I had been holding inside. In essence, I filled the containment field with an explosive discharge of Additive and Subtractive Magic linked together. Those two things don't mix. Without the containment field, it would probably have taken out this whole floor of the palace, possibly this whole wing."

"Did it catch them in time while they were still in our world? Did it kill them?" Kahlan asked, expectantly.

"Yes. That greasy black soot in there is all that's left of them. The goddess thought she had learned from Dori's mother that magic isn't anything to fear. I wanted to show her just how mistaken she was, so I unleashed my hate on those hateful creatures, the kind of hate that only a war wizard can unleash. I have only just begun to show them my wrath."

Berdine thrust a fist into the air. "Yes! That's my Lord Rahl."

The other Mord-Sith looked equally pleased, if less animated about it.

Kahlan leaned forward hopefully. "So, then

you were able to kill the Golden Goddess as well."

Richard looked from the Mord-Sith back to Kahlan as he slowly shook his head. "I killed the little girl who was hosting her. But the goddess wasn't really there, in her. It's something like the way the dream walkers used people. Remember when you once tried to kill the dream walker by touching someone he was using, but he was gone as soon as you unleashed your power? This was much the same. She was only using the girl to look through her eyes and use her voice. The goddess wasn't physically there, in Dori. I only had an instant to act when she gave Glee the command to take me or they would have all torn into me or escaped. I had no choice but to kill Dori along with all those hateful things."

He let out a long sigh. "But it accomplished two things. First, I learned that I don't believe that the goddess is able to enter the mind of a gifted person."

"Why do you think that?" Shale asked.

"Because she would have if she could have. As weak as Dori's mother's gift was, the goddess couldn't get into her mind. That is why she had to use Dori. That was as close as she could get."

"What's the second thing?" Kahlan asked.

"It takes them a second or two to materialize here, in our world. Then, when they get here, they have to grasp their surroundings, look for any threat, and take in their target. It's only an instant, but in that instant they are vulnerable.

"But to kill them after they were here and before they could escape back to their world, and more importantly to strike fear of us into the hearts of their kind through the eyes of the Golden Goddess, I had to kill Dori, too."

Kahlan put her arms around his neck, holding his head to her shoulder. "You had no choice, Richard. You had no choice."

"I know. I am *fuer grissa ost drauka*. I am the bringer of death."

21

"Are you sure they can't enter the mind of a person with magic?" Shale asked.

"I can't say I know that with absolute certainty," Richard told her, "but after talking to the goddess through Dori, I'm convinced that she isn't able to use the gifted—or she would already have done that. I believe she isn't able to enter our minds for the simple reason that her ability isn't compatible with our gift. Simply put, our gift won't allow her in."

Shale squinted with uncertainty. "Won't allow it?"

"While the goddess and the Glee can do what seems unfathomable to us—traveling to other worlds—I think that magic must block their ability to get past it and into our minds. That's why they were leery of the gift.

"They are predators. They hunt, which proves they have the ability to think and plan. And from the evidence of the dead we found down below, they work together. There are plenty of animals that are very dangerous, that stalk their prey and work together, but can't fathom magic. It stymies them."

"But you can't say with absolute certainty that they can't use the mind of the gifted," Shale pressed.

"Their primary goal is to eliminate me and Kahlan, right? So why not use you? If they could do it," Richard insisted, "then the goddess would have chosen to enter your mind, don't you suppose? You are close to me." He swept an arm around. "Or the mind of one of the Mord-Sith. They are even closer. If she was able to do that, then why choose a little girl? Because the minds of children are weaker, that's why," he said, answering his own question.

"But Nolo was an adult," Shale argued.

Richard smiled. "He was a diplomat, through and through. All of Nolo's people are bred to be diplomats, raised as diplomats."

Shale frowned. "So?"

"What adult mind is more simplistic and childlike than a diplomat's?"

Shale considered a moment. "I suppose you could be right."

"Killing me and Kahlan is her goal. When we're asleep, the Mord-Sith watch over us. If the goddess could use the mind of a gifted person, she would have already killed Kahlan and me by simply having a Mord-Sith do it while we were asleep. If she could have, she would have."

"I see your point," the sorceress conceded. She met his gaze. "Now that you mention it, as I said before, I had a murky vision of some kind of being when I was in meditation. It was just beyond awareness and I didn't know what it could be. That the vague, shadowy image had to be the goddess trying to make a connection with me, but ultimately failing. You have to be right that they can't enter the mind of the gifted or she would have entered my mind right then and there."

"So, then we have learned something useful," Kahlan said.

Richard flashed her a smile. "Yes, we have. It means we can use the gifted to help us without worrying that the goddess could be watching what we do through their eyes. But now we also know that anyone ungifted here at the palace could be an unwitting spy. That means that the goddess could even enter the mind of any of the First File." He arched an eyebrow. "Not exactly safe having them watch over us while we sleep."

Kahlan looked around at the decidedly unsettled looks on the faces of the Mord-Sith. "That's an alarming bit of news."

"Do you know where there are more gifted who could be helpful?" Shale asked. "All those here at the People's Palace may have enough of the gift to keep the goddess out of their minds, but they don't have enough power to be of any use in defeating these things."

"The Wizard's Keep," Vika answered in Richard's place.

"That's right," he said, nodding at her. "If we can get there, then—"

Everyone turned when they heard twin screams echo up a stairwell not far down the corridor. They were the kind of screams that could mean only one thing.

Every one of the Mord-Sith immediately swung the Agiel hanging on a fine gold chain from her wrist up into her fist as Richard broke into a dead run. All the Mord-Sith were right behind. Richard and the Mord-Sith beat the soldiers to the stairs, but not Kahlan and Shale.

Kahlan was not pleased to be stuck behind so many hulking men as Richard charged down the stairs. As they reached the next level down, a service area, Kahlan saw past the men and the railing that the torches were out, as were the lamps. The only light was that coming down the stairwell.

In the shadows, she could see a dark shape flailing away at someone already on the ground.

Still four steps from the bottom, Richard leaped off the stairs toward the shadowy shape of the threat. His sword came out in midair, sending its unique ring of steel down the dark hallway. The blade, steel blackened from touching the world of the dead, flashed as it came up into the air.

Richard, screaming with lethal intent, swung the sword with all his might while still in mid-leap. The blade whistled as it arced through the air. A black arm lifted in defense, only to be severed.

As Richard was landing on his feet, the dark

arm, with three massive claws at the end, spiraled through the air. At the same time, the rest of the creature turned back into scribbles as it vanished into thin air.

The Mord-Sith dove off the stairs after Richard, all of them striving to reach the threat. But it was gone before they could get to it. The Mord-Sith, along with the soldiers, charged off into the darkness, looking for any more of the Glee.

Two women were sprawled on their backs on the floor, clearly dead. The rib cage of one and the abdomen of the other had been ripped open almost to their spines by powerful strikes from those claws, leaving their insides spread across the floor.

Almost without pause, Richard stormed off down the hall right behind the soldiers, then sped past them, his sword in hand, hoping to catch more of the attackers.

Kahlan stood with Shale as the others raced away to make sure the dark hall was clear. Other soldiers collected torches and headed into the darkness. Shale leaned down to check, but it was obvious to Kahlan that no amount of healing would bring life back to the poor women. They were two of the palace staff, and had simply been going about their work when they had been cut down. Kahlan couldn't help thinking about their families. She wondered if they had children who would never see their mothers again.

As Shale looked up at Kahlan to say that nothing could be done, her eyes went wide. Kahlan realized that the sorceress was seeing something behind her. Without hesitation, Kahlan ducked and rolled to the side, just in time as claws swept past, flicking a lock of hair on the way by and barely missing catching her neck.

Shale thrust an arm out. From her hand a wavering glow to the air instantly left with a loud crack, like the crack of a whip. As Kahlan was rolling back to her feet, turning to face the enemy, the strike of Shale's power went right through the dark shape just as it was dissolving back into its own world. That magic hit a far wall and blew a hole through it, sending bits of plaster and stone flying everywhere. Kahlan could see the main corridor beyond through that hole.

She didn't know what sort of magic Shale had used. Kahlan had never seen anything quite like it. But then again, she had never seen a sorceress and a witch woman combined in one person.

Richard returned just as Shale rushed over to Kahlan to make sure she was all right.

"What happened?" he asked.

"One of them tried to get me," Kahlan said. "Shale saved me just in time. She tried to strike it down with her power"—Kahlan gestured to the hole in the wall—"but it was already vanishing and got away."

Kahlan and Richard were suddenly surrounded by Mord-Sith, but the threat had already passed. Soldiers closed in beyond the Mord-Sith, forming another ring of protection, swords all pointed outward.

"You're right," Shale told Richard. "They are thinking creatures. One of them attacked these two women to draw you away so that another could strike behind you at Kahlan."

Richard gritted his teeth in anger. "And I took the bait, leaving Kahlan unprotected." He thought better of what he said. "Except for you, of course. Thanks, Shale."

She offered a smile. "I just wish I had been faster. I almost had it. Next time I'll have to be quicker."

Richard sheathed his sword, helping to quench the anger in his eyes as he looked down at the arm on the ground. It had been severed cleanly just above the elbow, bone and all. Its skin was as he had described it—almost black, smooth, and slimy. The blood was red. The bloody claw, with strings of tissue and clothes stuck in it from the two women it had killed, slowly closed and opened once in death before finally going still.

Kahlan was enraged that it had murdered the two women, and another one of them almost had its claws into her. "If I would have just been a second faster, I could have touched it with my power after it took that swing at me."

"Well," Shale said, "at least one of them went back without an arm. That's a good message to send back to them."

Richard didn't look pleased. "A message that will likely anger them. From what you said about there being killings in the Northern Waste, and other reports we've had, the Glee are randomly attacking people everywhere.

"But it's becoming clear that their main focus is to attack people around Kahlan and me in an effort to draw us into making a mistake. The goddess is becoming obsessed with killing you and me," he said to Kahlan. "They almost got you for a second time. We can't let that happen again. We have to deny them their plan while I try to figure out a way to end the threat."

"How?" Kahlan asked.

Richard ran his fingers back through his hair. "Everyone in our world is now in danger from the Glee, but the people here at the palace are in much greater danger because we're here. They are going to be targeted, just like these two women were, simply to try to draw us into making a mistake. As long as we're here at the palace, this place is going to be a killing field.

"Besides that, the goddess could be looking at us through the eyes of anyone in the palace." He passed a brief look over the soldiers with their backs to them, swords pointed out toward any threat. His meaning was obvious. The goddess could even be using one of the men of the First File. "It's too dangerous for the people here at the palace for us to be here, and it's too dangerous for us to be here. We need to leave.

"If we leave, the focus of the Glee will be to come after us. We need to draw them away from all these innocent people."

Kahlan's brow lifted with a sudden idea. She leaned in and spoke quietly so that the soldiers wouldn't hear in case the goddess was listening through one of them.

"We can leave in the sliph. In a way, the sliph enables us to do something like the Glee. It allows us to travel to a different place in our world in a very short time. Traveling in the sliph will get us far away from here and draw the attention of the goddess away from all these people. That kind of departure might even confuse the goddess."

Richard smiled at her. "Exactly. We need to leave at once."

"But go where?" Kahlan asked.

Richard's smile broadened. "To someplace with gifted who do have lots of power. We need to get to the Wizard's Keep. There are gifted there—real gifted. The Sisters of the Light are there, as are other gifted they are training."

"What are Sisters of the Light?" Shale asked, keeping an eye toward any soldier who might be listening.

"Sorceresses," he said before turning back to Kahlan. "We need to leave at once, before there are more attacks here and before the goddess can get one of us. If we leave in the sliph, that will confuse the goddess as to where we went and hopefully buy us some time."

22

Kahlan stuffed some of her things into a backpack on the bed as Richard did the same. They needed to get out of the People's Palace to confuse the Golden Goddess and lead the Glee away from all the innocent people there.

Kahlan was cautiously excited about being at the safety of the Wizard's Keep. Not only were there a lot of gifted people there, the Keep itself was filled with all kinds of protective shields. Any of the Glee that the goddess sent there would be in danger without realizing it. There were lethal shields in any number of places throughout the Keep that would incinerate anything that didn't belong there or have the proper magic to allow safe passage. The whole Keep would be a death trap for the Glee.

For the first time in days, Kahlan felt a glimmer of hope.

The Keep would also be a place of safety for her to have their children.

Once they were safely in the Keep and it would soon become obvious, Kahlan would finally be able to tell Richard that she was pregnant with twins. They would be safe there, with Sisters of the Light and others to protect her. The Keep had protective magic to protect from invasions. The whole purpose of the Keep was to protect the First Wizard and the gifted working there.

At the Keep, Richard would be able to figure out a way to stop the goddess. Kahlan didn't know why she hadn't thought of the Keep sooner.

The Wizard's Keep was also Richard's other ancestral home. The People's Palace had always been the seat of power for the House of Rahl, but the Wizard's Keep had always been the ancestral home to the First Wizard. It was his Keep. Part of its purpose was to protect him.

If it was safe enough to leave the Keep, Kahlan could possibly give birth to their children at the nearby Confessors' Palace, where she had been born. That was her ancestral home. There were people there who had known Kahlan since she had been born. If it was safe enough to leave the Keep, her dream would be to have her children at the Confessors' Palace. The daughters of a Confessor were always Confessors, so Kahlan would dearly love to have her daughter be born at the Confessors' Palace. The twins could then be raised in the safety of the Keep.

As a young girl, Kahlan had spend a great deal of time in the Keep, under the watchful eye of wizards. The Keep was a place of power for the First Wizard. It would protect his children. And, in turn, those children would continue their lines of magic to protect their world. That would bring life back to the Wizard's Keep the way it had been alive when she had been a girl.

Both she and Richard changed out of their official clothes and into their traveling clothes. Richard put some of his war-wizard outfit in his pack, but kept on the black shirt, the special weapons belt, and the broad, leather-padded, silver wristbands with ancient symbols in the language of Creation. Kahlan didn't need to pack her Mother Confessor's dress, because the Confessors' Palace was there in Aydindril, near the Keep. She had other dresses of the Mother

Confessor there, all the same silky fabric, all with the same square-cut neckline.

Her whole life she had grown up wearing the black dresses that all Confessors wore. Only the woman chosen by her sister Confessors wore the white dress of the Mother Confessor. Kahlan had been the youngest woman ever named Mother Confessor. It was a testament to the strength of her power.

When she and Richard emerged from their bedroom, all six Mord-Sith, all in red leather, were waiting out in the round entryway along with Shale. Each of the Mord-Sith had a small pack with her. Shale was dressed in her black traveling clothes with a black cloak draped over her shoulders and held together at the top with bone buttons connected by a short silver chain. She had her pack with her as well.

They were all obviously intending to go with Richard and Kahlan. That was fine with Kahlan, and she knew it would be with Richard, too. Of course, their wishes were irrelevant, because the Mord-Sith would have already decided that they were going.

Importantly, the goddess couldn't use them or Shale, so the Mord-Sith would be fearless guardians of her children. Kahlan was grateful that they were coming along to the Keep.

A large force of the First File, Lieutenant Dolan in command, waited off a ways in the wide corridor. With what had happened in the containment-field library, as well as the two women being murdered, to say nothing of the horrific discovery down in the lower reaches of the palace, the men all looked grim and tense. Kahlan couldn't help looking to see if any of them averted their eyes. None did.

"We need to get down to the sliph," Richard told Berdine confidentially, so that the soldiers wouldn't overhear. "I don't want anyone but us nine knowing where we are going."

She nodded. "I know a fast route. It will also keep us out of sight."

Richard nodded to her and then went down the hall a short distance to meet the man in command. "Lieutenant, I need to leave on an important mission."

The man tipped his head. "Of course, Lord Rahl. How many men do you want to take with you?"

"None. Right now I'm in too much of a hurry." At the look on the man's face, he added,

"I will send for some of the First File when I can. In the meantime, you know the threat here at the palace. You know how dangerous these creatures are. As you saw, they bleed, so they can be killed if you can catch them in time before they can vanish."

The lieutenant looked uneasy. "While you were getting your things, there was another attack back not far away in one of the hallways branching from this corridor. Two of my men were killed."

The muscles in Richard's jaw flexed in anger.

"They need to eliminate Kahlan and me so that they can rampage unrestrained across our world, hunting our species to extinction. That's one reason we need to leave. By leaving I hope to confuse them. Since they are focused on us, the sooner we leave the palace, the less the danger to the people here. At least for now.

"Tell Mr. Burkett that the Lord Rahl has had to leave on an important mission. The man is used to taking care of the palace while the Lord Rahl is gone. He will know what to do. Help him in any way you can."

"I will see to it, Lord Rahl."

"With Kahlan and me gone, the First File will

be the only protection for the people here at the palace. I don't want any of the First File to leave the palace for any reason. I'm counting on you and the First File to stand here in my place and protect everyone. I will be the magic against magic, doing what is necessary to end the threat."

Lieutenant Dolan, looking resolute, clapped a fist to the leather armor over his heart.

"The Mord-Sith will protect us from here on out. You and the men must see to protecting the people here."

The man reluctantly saluted again, tapping his fist to his heart.

Richard turned to Berdine. "Let's go."

23

Berdine immediately started down the corridor. The ranks of heavily armed men in the corridor all moved to the sides of the broad passageway for her and her charges. Nyda went in front with Berdine. Kahlan, holding Richard's hand, was next, with Vika right behind her. Shale, Rikka, Vale, and Cassia took up the rear guard.

The entire way past all the soldiers to either side of the corridor, all standing with their backs to the wall to make room, Kahlan met the eyes of each man in turn. There was not one who averted their gaze. That much of it was a relief. She hoped they could escape the People's Palace without the Golden Goddess seeing them leaving through someone's eyes. As she had learned as a little girl being taught combat strategy by her father, King Wyborn, confusing the enemy was always a valuable tactic.

Berdine led them at a near run down side halls and narrow stairwells and through a labyrinth of dark and deserted passageways as they wound their way ever lower and across the restricted section of the palace. Everyone followed in silence. They all knew the dangers they were leaving behind and the ones they might encounter along the way. They watched for any threats as they moved as silently as possible.

Kahlan was excited to finally have a plan that she knew could work. The Sisters of the Light could be overbearing and full of themselves at times, but they were loyal to Richard and to life. They had fought valiantly in the war. She was confident they would face this new threat with determination and grit.

Kahlan wished so much, as she had so many times, that Richard's grandfather were still with them. Zedd had been an important part of her life ever since she met him. He had watched over her in ways that no other could. The wily old wizard had wormed his way into her heart from the first. But in a way, with Richard, she still had part of Zedd with her.

With a great sense of relief, they finally reached the sliph's room without being seen or being attacked. Kahlan had feared that the goddess would somehow try to stop them. But with only the Mord-Sith and Shale with them, there had been no eyes able to watch where they went, rendering the goddess blind. While the protection of the First File would be valuable, the risk of having the goddess see or hear what they were doing through one of them was now too great.

Without delay, Richard crossed the ancient room to the waist-high, round wall of the massive well. He leaned over the stone cap and put the silver wristbands together at his wrists. They began to glow brighter until Kahlan could see the shadows of his bones right through his flesh.

"Sliph!" he called down into the darkness. "I need you!" His voice echoed up from the well and around the domed room.

Shale looked especially tense, not knowing what to expect. Kahlan twisted her fingers together, worried that maybe the sliph might not come, or maybe she wasn't even there anymore. Shale, now knowing what Richard was doing, gave Kahlan a puzzled frown. Kahlan thought it would be best for her to wait and see it for herself.

As they waited in silence, pebbles and dirt on the stone floor started dancing as a vibration rose up from deep below. With building intensity, the whole room reverberated with a droning rumble. Dust fell from joints in the stone walls and domed ceiling.

With a roar of tremendous speed the silver sliph shot up from the depths of her well, stopping abruptly at the top rather than surging out. The silvery, liquid surface calmed, and then a lump of it rose up into the air. A beautiful silver face formed. A silver arm reached out and cupped Richard's face.

"Master, it is good to see you again," she said in her beguiling voice. "Come, we will travel. You will be pleased."

Richard held an arm back to the rest of them waiting by the wall. "We all need to travel. We need to go right away."

For the first time, it seemed, the sliph looked around and saw that there were eight women with him, or possibly she'd seen them before and

simply didn't care about anyone but Richard.
Now that she thought about it, Kahlan realized
that was probably it. She fumed silently at the
way the sliph smiled at Richard.

"All of you wish to travel?"

"Yes," Richard hurriedly said for everyone, as
he motioned with an arm to urge them all closer.
"We all need to travel. I would be very pleased if
you would take us all. We're in a hurry."

Shale, looking quite alarmed, took a step
back.

"Where do you wish to travel?" the sliph
asked in that silky, silvery voice that for some
reason grated on Kahlan's nerves.

"The Keep," Richard said. "I would be very
pleased if you would take us all to the Wizard's
Keep."

"I know the place," she cooed to him. "I can
take you there. But you know you can't take
that sword." She slipped her arm around behind
him in a familiar way to touch the scabbard.

Richard pressed his lips tight for a moment.
"I know. I'll have to leave it here until we can
return."

He pulled the baldric off over his head.
"Now that the blade has touched death," he

told Kahlan, "I think I could take it, but with so much at stake, I fear to risk it." He leaned the scabbard up against the stone wall.

Kahlan didn't like the idea of him leaving the sword, but she remembered how in the past taking it with him nearly cost him his life. He was right, there was too much at stake.

"Come closer," the sliph said to everyone, her voice more businesslike, not nearly as soft and smooth as when she spoke to Richard.

All the Mord-Sith approached to stand before the stone wall of the well. The sliph's silver arm reached out, her fingers gently passing from one to another, brushing each forehead briefly.

"You all have what is required to travel."

Richard hooked Shale's arm under his and pulled her closer. Her eyes were wide with shock at seeing the sliph and hearing it speak. Such a creature, created by ancient wizards, was obviously something she had never encountered before, and she was more than a little wary of it. It had to be incomprehensible to her.

"Is this safe?" she whispered to Richard.

"It is for me," the sliph said with a smooth, silvery smile before sliding her silver fingers across Shale's smooth brow. Shale winced but stood her ground. The sliph pulled her hand back. "She cannot travel. She doesn't have the required magic."

"What is she talking about?" said Shale with sudden displeasure. "I'm a sorceress. I have the gift. Obviously, I have magic."

Richard shook his head. "You misunderstand. You need both Additive and Subtractive Magic to travel in the sliph."

Shale took a step back. "Subtractive Magic? Are you crazy?"

Richard waved a hand to dismiss her concern as he climbed up to stand on the stone wall. "I can give you enough of it to make it possible for you to travel. Don't worry. I've done it before."

As Richard was reassuring Shale, the sliph reached out to run a hand across Kahlan's brow.

"She may not travel," the silver face announced with a hint of distaste.

Richard had just helped Vika up beside him. He turned to frown at the sliph, then held an arm out toward Kahlan. "What are you talking about? Kahlan has traveled before many times. Of course she can travel."

"Not now."

Richard growled his impatience. "Why not?"

"Because she is pregnant. She and the two babies growing in her would die in me if she were to try to travel."

Richard turned with a look that locked Kahlan's breath in her lungs. Richard stood frozen with a look of shock on his face as he stared down at her. She suddenly felt hot all over. Her fingers and toes tingled. She thought she might pass out.

Kahlan forced herself to speak. "It's all right, Richard. You and Vika go. I will stay here. Shale and my sisters of the Agiel will protect me. I will have your sword. You must travel to the Keep to get help. You must. It's our only chance."

Richard hadn't moved a muscle as he stared at her. The room rang with a terrible silence. No one said a word.

The Mord-Sith were all staring at her, but Kahlan could only look into Richard's gray eyes.

She swallowed again, desperately trying to hold back tears as she took a step back away from the sliph's well. "I love you. Now go."

The story continues.

Episode 3 of the Children of D'Hara

WASTELAND

coming soon...